Lainie,

I know we haven't spoken much in the past few years, but you have to come back to the ranch. Tess is your sister, too, and since her parents—your mother and my father—are gone now, I can't deal with her coming-of-age by myself. You're a woman, so maybe she'll relate to you better. She sure isn't listening to me.

I also know we both experienced some confusing feelings before you left. But we were in our late teens, just out of childhood ourselves. Now Tess is what's important, so we'll have to put that attraction aside. After this many years, we both should have put it behind us anyway.

So please return as soon as possible. Tess needs you. I need you.

Sincerely,

Dev

Dear Reader,

I just love stories about going home and finding some new and wonderful thing there. When my folks come out to California to visit with my family, I take them on my grand San Francisco tour, which includes a trip down Lombard Street, billed as the "crookedest street in the world," and one down Filbert, which is the "steepest urban street in the world," and on to Alcatraz and the Golden Gate Bridge. My sister complained that she had nothing so great in the farmland of Kentucky to show me.

Nothing great? Only about fifty of my favorite relatives and the same number in my hubby's family to exchange hugs and news with. My folks consult with his, and they plan family get-togethers on different days so my gang can attend both! And then there's the homemade ice cream and the most heavenly hot fudge sauce, plus peanut butter cookies from Aunt Ottie...hmm, my absolute favorites. We bring pictures and share stories of the latest grandkids. Oh, and I love the wedding pictures and welcoming new nieces, nephews and cousins into the family. I insist they tell me how they met and give me all the romantic details. And they do!

I'm getting all teary-eyed just thinking about it. Excuse me while I grab a tissue. Let's see, where was I? Oh, yes, there was this heroine who returned home after being away for a long time....

Laurie Paige

LAURIE PAIGE

A Season for Homecoming

Published by Silhouette Books

America's Publisher of Contemporary Romance

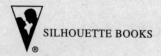

SILHOUETTE BOOKS

ISBN-13: 978-0-373-36147-2
ISBN-10:   0-373-36147-5

A SEASON FOR HOMECOMING

Copyright © 1990 by Olivia M. Hall

Visit Silhouette Books at www.eHarlequin.com

Printed in U.S.A.

LAURIE PAIGE

"One of the nicest things about writing romances is researching locales, careers and ideas. In the interest of authenticity, most writers will try anything… once." Along with her writing adventures, Laurie has been a NASA engineer, a past president of the Romance Writers of America—she is also a mother and a grandmother. She was twice a Romance Writers of America RITA® Award finalist for Best Traditional Romance and has won awards from *Romantic Times BOOKreviews* for Best Silhouette Special Edition and Best Silhouette, in addition to appearing on the *USA TODAY* bestseller list. Recently resettled in Northern California, Laurie is looking forward to whatever experiences her next novel will send her on.

Chapter One

"You're not leaving the house looking like that."

"Yes, I am! There's nothing wrong with the way I look!"

Lainie Alder paused in the act of hanging up her favorite silk blouse and wished she had paid heed to the misgivings she had felt upon arriving. If she had she would have quietly stolen away before the quarreling duo on the patio below her window knew she was there.

Coward, she chided herself. She had arrived at the ranch only a half hour ago. She hung the blouse in the closet. Pushing a strand of wavy black hair off her forehead, she closed her eyes and tried to shut out the angry voices—Dev's, dark and dangerous; Tess', strident and defensive.

For a second Lainie heard other angry voices rising out of the painful mists of her own past, when she had been sixteen like Tess—young and hurt. She had so wanted the approval of the Garrick men at that age. She had wanted to be a part of them…to be loved by them.

Sudden tears burned her eyes, startling her. Perhaps she shouldn't have returned to the ranch just yet. The memories were still painful. How could they have the power to wound as if they had occurred yesterday?

Shoving the past aside she hooked the wispy strand of hair behind her ear and prepared to step into the fray. After all, that was the reason she had been summoned to the ranch.

The phone call she had received from her stepbrother, Devlin Garrick, two weeks ago at her town house in Virginia Beach had been definite about what was expected of her. "Get out here and do something with her before I break her neck," he said. "She's your sister, too."

She had referred to Tess Garrick, child of the marriage between Dev's father, Charles, and Lainie's mother, Debra, and therefore half sister to both Dev and Lainie.

Lainie descended the stairs and paused on the bottom step, feeling guilty for her neglect of Tess. Then she dismissed the emotion. Not one month had passed in all the years since she'd moved away that she hadn't written or called her beloved younger sister. From the day she had left for boarding school shortly before her seventeenth birthday to the present, she had faithfully kept in touch.

Besides, Dev hadn't mentioned any problems in their infrequent correspondence, so why would she have suspected any? She still wasn't sure what the difficulty was, except that Dev refused to "shoulder the responsibility alone" anymore. He had demanded that she do her share.

"You're a woman. Maybe you can talk to her. I sure as hell can't," he said. "You'd better get out here before there's real trouble."

After such a charming invitation, how could she refuse? she questioned wryly, attempting to take a lighter view of the situation.

As Lainie approached the open doors to the patio she heard Tess cry in outrage, "I do not look like a floozy! We're supposed to dress like this. It's a *tacky* dance."

Upon hearing this declaration Lainie was prepared for the worst, but Tess' clothes weren't half as bad as she expected. Tess was wearing high-heeled sandals with pink knee socks scrunched around her ankles. Her hot pink pants clashed brightly with an orange blouse tied in a knot at the waist. A row of rainbow-hued plastic bracelets jangled on one arm.

"Lainie!" Tess squealed, seeing her in the doorway.

Lainie experienced a sharp stab of protective love for Tess. It seemed such a short time ago that her mother had let her hold and feed the new baby. Now that baby was nearly a woman.

Tess was looking at her with surprise and delight on her young face—from what Lainie could see of it.

The teenager's light brown eyes were highlighted with coral shadow. A pink vinyl rose clung to one cheek, and a gigantic orange earring was attached to an earlobe. Her tawny brown hair was secured with a pink butterfly clip just above her left temple. Ironically, she looked more wholesome than tacky.

"Oh, Lainie, Dev won't let me go to the end-of-school dance. He's being horrible and mean." Every utterance was a wail of despair. Her eyes threw darts toward her brother.

Lainie turned to Dev. A tremor ran through her as she faced him in person for the first time in over a year. He had always had a tremendous impact on her.

"Hello, Lainie," he said. His expression indicated that he thought it was about time she showed up.

"Hello," she said, just as cool as he had been.

He leaned against the rock wall that separated the patio from the yard. His hands were jammed into his jeans pockets, his legs stretched in front of him, one ankle crossed over the other. A work shirt hung open revealing flesh bronzed by days in the Arizona sun. Whorls of dark chest hair glinted with golden highlights in the late afternoon light, inviting the playful caress of fingertips through the wiry curls.

A breeze toyed with his shirttail, then riffled the dark brown hair that fell over his forehead. His manner was calm, his pose relaxed, but Lainie wasn't deceived. The tension in his lean frame was visible in the set of his shoulders. He stood with one smooth motion and came to her.

She was engulfed by the man-smell of him—of dust and horses and the sweat of hard work done in the warm June air. It upset her equilibrium. It almost made her dizzy. It certainly made her think of things other than quarreling.

"Is Tess on restriction?" she asked when he stopped no more than a foot away. His brown eyes, clear as cider, flicked over her wobbly smile. He was very angry.

"I didn't say she couldn't go to the dance, just that she couldn't go looking like that." His eyes condemned the outfit.

"He wants me to go looking like…like something out of a museum!" Tess said, glaring at him, the set of her chin as stubborn as his. Each bore the stamp of Charles Garrick in facial structure, in hair and eye color, and in temper.

Dev laughed briefly at this declaration. Lainie witnessed the stab of wounded pride in Tess' eyes before the girl crossed her arms over her chest and stared past the paddocks toward the mountains. She remembered her own aching desire for a word of affection and encouragement at that age.

The laughter left no trace on Dev's stern face. "I doubt if even a museum of modern art would accept that getup."

Lainie schooled herself to remain outwardly calm. "Why not?" she asked. "I think it looks charming."

The simultaneous gapes of surprise on their faces would have been comical if Lainie had felt like laughing, but her sympathy was aroused on her sister's behalf. She inquired in a gentler tone, "It's a theme dance, you said?"

"Yes," Tess said. "We're *supposed* to look tacky."

"Well, you certainly do," Lainie said. She cast Dev a smiling glance, inviting him to relent. "Dev apparently agrees, judging by his reaction."

His eyes swept over Lainie's traveling suit of navy blue. "I doubt if any of your clothes look like that," he said, a hard edge returning to his voice. "You have more sense."

Lainie wanted to ask what sense had to do with anything when a person was searching for an identity, wanting to be in fashion and probably trying to impress some young man, all at the same time? Instead she said softly, her voice soothing, "You're behind the times. Beads and bangles are in this year."

They heard a car on the drive, then the sound of the doorbell.

"Robbie's here. I have to go." Although her glance was defiant, Tess hesitated before attempting to leave.

Lainie met Dev's glare without flinching.

"You'd let her go out in those clothes with all that junk on her face?" he finally asked.

Lainie nodded. "Unless you have other reasons…?"

The two females watched him while he considered. At least he made up his mind. "All right, but you be home one hour after the dance is over," he warned Tess.

"I will!" Tess beamed as she kissed each of them, then rushed for the patio door. "Oh, welcome home, Lainie."

She was gone with a click of three-inch heels on the patio stones, leaving a trail of sweet perfume and total silence behind her. Lainie gazed after Tess, considering the difference between them. Tess was open in her feelings, quick to tears or laughter, while Lainie had learned to hide her own emotions. Life, she had found, was easier that way.

Dev pivoted on one foot forcing Lainie to shift back a little to meet his gaze. He stood seven inches taller than her five feet, six inches, but he seemed much more than that all at once. She recognized the control he was exerting over his temper in the deepening lines at the corners of his mouth. She also saw that he was tired.

It was a new observation and it drew conflicting

feelings from her, a softening of her guard and an inclination to wariness at the same time.

"Where are your bangles?" he asked. "Or pink pants that look as if you have to be poured into them?"

His voice deliberately trailed off as his gaze went to a point on her thighs, burning right through the crinkled linen of her suit. She nearly gasped aloud at the fierce heat that flared in the pit of her abdomen.

"No wonder you and Tess are having battles, if that's the way you treat her," she said with outward poise. She paced away from him, then swung around with her hands on her hips. "How can you be so blind to her needs?"

"Her needs? What the hell are you talking about?" he asked. "She looked like a...like she was on her way to an evening's work." He covered the distance between them in three long strides that effectively had him looming over her again.

Lainie refused to retreat. "She looked like a teenager who's trying to move from girl to woman and isn't sure of the process. You should have given her assurance instead of yelling at her."

"Assurance of what?"

"Assurance that, in your opinion as a male, she's attractive as a female. She needed your approval."

"What man in his right mind would approve that ridiculous outfit?" he demanded. "If you think—"

Lainie cut him off. "She wants to be noticed.

Can't you see that? Do you have to be so insensitive?''

"Insensitive?'' he echoed, his voice going soft.

Lainie clenched her hands to hold them steady. He studied her with his head tilted slightly, his gaze oblique. She watched him while the anger dissipated and was replaced with another emotion not so easily read. She had never been able to read his thoughts… except once.

"Yes, insensitive,'' she continued quietly. "You're the prominent male in her life. Tess naturally looks to you to guide her and give her clues on what traits appeal to men.''

Just as she had wanted his approval in her tender days, she realized. Why did it hurt so much to remember?

The heartaches of the young never fade. That was why she was defending Tess so insistently. Lately, Lainie had detected a note of unhappiness in Tess' brief letters. She had to make Dev see how much Tess needed his warm, loving approbation.

"Well, all that goop on her face isn't one of them.'' He reached out and swiped a thumb over Lainie's lips. "You don't wear much makeup.''

Lainie's breath caught in her throat. Her pulse beat a hard rat-a-tat-tat. She stared at Dev, fragile emotion perilously near the surface. It was only a casual touch, she reminded herself, not a lover's caress.

She focused her attention on his face until she was

once more in control, then she tried to assess him rationally.

He was a handsome man. She had thought so the first time she saw him when Charles had brought his new wife and her sixteen-year-old daughter home to the ranch. Dev had been eighteen then. Now he was thirty-five and she was thirty-three. It was time to get over the pangs of youth...when she had thought she was in love with him.

"You didn't wear much as a teenager, either. You never seemed to go through the fads that all the other girls did." His hand lingered, the tips of his fingers under her chin. "Why didn't you, Lainie?" he asked.

She pulled away. "Because my father knew how to make a female feel she was perfect without any additional help."

"Your father deserted you and Debra when you were hardly out of diapers," Dev reminded her, his voice low and harsh. The unreadable expression left his eyes, and his face was stern once more.

"Not deserted. He kept in touch after the divorce." She inhaled deeply, breathing in the essence of Dev, all the warm, earthy scents she identified with him.

She fought an aching impulse to rest her head on the inviting expanse of his chest and slip her arms beneath his open shirt so she could clasp the firm flesh of his waist. She had her own needs, she realized, the needs of a woman. No, she mustn't think about that. She was here to help with Tess.

Quickly, before the temptation to touch him had time to grow, she turned toward the house. "I need to finish my unpacking."

"Lainie," he said impatiently, an unspoken order for her to stay in his voice. She continued into the house.

In her room she saw that her hands were trembling. There were reasons she hadn't wanted to come back here, she thought. Dev was one of them.

The breeze stirred the lace curtain at the window. She walked over to it and stared at the landscape.

The house stood on a gentle rise above the flatness of the valley, out of reach of the wash filled with spring runoff that meandered through a belt of cottonwoods. A hill hunkered close behind the dwelling like a protective lover, its shoulders of mauve-brown dirt and red rock sloping into an irregular embrace on the north and south.

The fresh green of late spring clung delicately to the hills. Near the house Arizona sage and yellow lupine formed thick clumps of vegetation in contrast to the river gravel that took the place of a front lawn.

Mother's doing, Lainie thought, recalling her parent's love of gardening. Debra had made the landscape around the home lovely and interesting by using patterns of rock and natural flora. Firs, pines and sycamores were planted for shade, native shrubs for color all around the spacious yard.

An airstrip had been laid out on the hardpan that formed a narrow ledge above the wash. A Piper was

tied down at the end. Lainie could have had Dev pick
her up at the commercial airport, but she had hired
old Mr. Grover to drive her out from Clarkdale. She
had wanted to see the land in a more intimate way
than was possible from the air. She had wanted to
reacquaint herself with it slowly, on her own, without
Dev or Tess to observe her. She hadn't been sure she
could guard her emotions.

Memories crowded her mind while she finished
putting her clothing away. After paying the driver,
who kindly carried her bags up the six broad steps
to the porch, she had faced the front door, aware of
the rapid beating of her heart. It had been well over
a year since she had last visited.

The ranch house was a stone-and-timber structure
that looked as solidly rooted to the ground as the
giant sycamore that shaded its front and the ridge that
protected its back. It was built on two levels. The
lower level contained the living and dining rooms,
kitchen and ranch office; the upper had three bedrooms and a common bathroom plus a master suite
with its own luxurious bath-dressing room, which
had been put in for her mother by Charles. Dev's
room now, she realized. She folded a sweater and
laid it in a drawer.

When she had entered the house she had almost
expected to see her mother rise gracefully from the
long sofa in the living room and rush to her, her
blond hair bouncing with soft curls, her face lit in a
smile wide and welcoming....

Lainie pushed the irritating strand of hair from her pale face and inhaled sharply, filled with remorse that she had seen so little of her mother in the years after college.

There had been her marriage to Conrad and her gift boutique in Virginia Beach. After establishing the business, she had traveled all over the world looking for unique items for the store. She had rarely had time for more than a long weekend visit to Arizona once or twice a year.

After her mother's death Lainie had visited even less. She had returned for a birthday party for Tess and once for her stepfather's funeral. He had had a heart attack three winters ago. Then there had been the long months of watching her own husband battle a little known disease that had slowly destroyed his life. She'd stopped by briefly for Christmas eighteen months ago.

So what had been her excuse since then? Would she be here now if not for the call from Dev demanding that she take on some of the responsibility for Tess?

No, she acknowledged. Some wiser part of her had known what to expect and had warned her away. She should have heeded it.

She changed to cotton pants and a sleeveless top, then slipped into sandals and went downstairs to see if Agnes, the housekeeper, had returned. No one had been available to greet her when she had arrived. So much for a warm welcome. Fortunately, it wasn't something she had anticipated.

After crossing the foyer to the kitchen she found the house still empty. She walked to the window and peered at the garden. Agnes was there, picking vegetables.

A commotion in the paddock drew her attention. Dev was schooling a young stallion. The horse was frisky and playful. It challenged his authority by darting at him, then veering away at the last moment. He flicked it with the tip of a training whip. The young horse stopped its prancing as if stunned by the light blow. He realized this was serious.

Lainie suddenly knew why she hadn't returned after her husband's death. She was much too vulnerable, not just to the past and its memories, but to the present, too. To Dev…his strength, his dominating masculinity…the gentleness she knew he possessed. If she ever needed a shoulder to cry on, he would supply it.

She stirred restlessly. Not pity, she couldn't bear that. What then? No answer occurred to her as she gazed out the window.

Dev guided the horse around the paddock, teaching him the proper responses for the show ring. It was beautiful to watch.

He had removed his shirt and hung it over the fence post. The wind waved it like a banner and tousled the thick, glossy hair of the man and the dark brown mane of the horse before rushing up the steep slope to tickle the leaves of the aspen trees.

In both man and animal, muscles tensed and relaxed as they went through the paces. Dev's expression was stern, as usual. As he grew older, the joy of life seemed to seep out of him, Lainie thought; yet, on occasion, she had seen him truly smile. His smile was enough to melt ice.

Lainie thought of how much he and Tess looked like Charles with their clean, sharp bone structure and honey-brown coloring. She carried the imprint of her father—his blue eyes and black hair, the widow's peak topping an angular face, pale skin that was hard to tan. Neither she nor Tess looked like their mother.

Agnes, swinging a basket of fresh greens, paused in the yard. She called something to Dev who answered, "In about an hour." Lainie assumed that the exchange had to do with dinner and realized she was hungry. She hadn't eaten much on the plane.

Glancing at the clock on the stove she saw that it was almost seven. Agnes liked to serve dinner, clean the kitchen, then go to her own house in time to watch her favorite television programs. She, too, was a widow.

When Agnes approached the back door, Lainie opened it for her. "Hi. Got enough for another salad?" she asked, peering in the basket at the fresh vegetables.

Agnes was somewhere between forty and sixty.

She had few lines and no gray hair. She had looked the same for the twenty years she had been at the Garrick ranch—neither plump nor thin, short or tall. Her manner was not effusive but neither was it distant. She studied Lainie with friendly gray eyes.

"Don't they have food back East?" she asked in her straightforward manner. "Or don't you remember to eat it?"

"I eat," Lainie protested with a laugh and a catch in her throat. Agnes was always the same. Her job was to keep the house neat and the occupants fed. She did both skillfully.

"You drive in?"

"I hired Mr. Grover to bring me out."

"Dev would have picked you up in Phoenix." There was a slight scold in her voice.

Lainie had been careful to accept few favors from the Garrick men. It made life simpler. "I caught the cargo shuttle into town. I wasn't certain what time my plane would get in. We were late taking off."

"He wouldn't have minded," Agnes said firmly. She gave Lainie a shrewd glance as if she knew exactly why Lainie hadn't asked.

When Charles and Debra had married Lainie had been thrilled to have a family. She had loved the ranch and her stepbrother on sight. It had been a few weeks before she understood that her stepfather could barely stand to look at her and longer before she realized that her presence was cause for argument between him and her mother. When she had become

aware of these painful truths, she had asked to go
back East to a boarding school she picked out of a
magazine and had spent little time with her mother
thereafter.

It was only as an adult that Lainie had realized she
had been a daily reminder of her father, the man who
had married Debra on the rebound after a lovers'
quarrel between her and Charles.

Lainie sighed. Her parents' marriage had ended in
divorce after four years, but by then Charles had married and had a son. A year after his wife died, Debra
returned to Clarkdale for a class reunion. She and
Charles had married within a month. It had seemed
impossibly romantic at the time.

"Here," Agnes said, putting a bowl of cantaloupe
on the oak table. "Eat this while supper's cooking."

"Thanks. Did you raise these?"

"No, they take up too much space. Dev wouldn't
plow any extra." At Lainie's surprised glance the
housekeeper continued, "Zed got down in his back
this spring, so Dev took over. Did Zed's chores and
ran the ranch, too."

"He's never seemed to mind any kind of work,"
Lainie murmured, remembering the times she had
watched him muck out the stables, or help birth a
foal or calf.

"No, not an ounce of arrogance in him," Agnes
agreed.

Lainie raised her brows at this. Maybe he wasn't
arrogant, but he was certainly opinionated. For Tess'

sake, she intended to make some changes in his attitude.

When she got a chance and when they were alone and he was feeling mellow, she would discuss the situation very calmly, one adult to another, and make him see the error of his ways. That was the way to handle things. Then she could leave.

She finished the fruit. "Is there anything I can do?" she asked, putting the bowl in the dishwasher.

"No, thanks. I can manage. There's a new magazine on the coffee table in the office."

That was Agnes' polite way of shooing her out of the kitchen, and Lainie took the hint.

She turned on the evening news with the remote control and settled on the sofa in the ranch office with a copy of *Better Homes and Gardens*. Starting from the back she flipped through it, mostly looking at the pictures.

Dev came in while she was reading an article. He paused at the door when he saw her, then went to the telephone. She pushed the volume button until no sound issued from Peter Jennings' lips. Concentrating on the newscaster's mouth, she tried to figure out what he was saying. Dev's voice interfered.

"Harper? Dev. My sister is at the dance for the juniors. Would you make sure she's there…she's with Bob Morley's boy…Thanks…Yeah…Keep an eye on things…Appreciate it."

By the time he hung up Lainie was shaking with

fury. Giving the magazine a fling that sent it flying across the coffee table to land on the floor, she jumped up and turned on Dev.

"Why didn't you just send a bodyguard with her? Or a baby-sitter. Better yet, why didn't you go to the dance yourself so you could make sure no one came within a hundred feet of Tess?"

He cast her a cool glance. "Harper can handle it." His tone said he wasn't in a mood to listen to her. Lainie ignored the warning signals.

"Why don't you just have her arrested?" Lainie demanded. "I can't believe you. Sending a deputy sheriff to check on her. It's beyond belief."

"It's necessary," he countered.

"Why? She's done nothing to warrant such a reaction. Her clothes and makeup aren't that bad—"

"You know nothing about it. You're never here to see what's going on, so don't give me any static on my actions." His glance was enigmatic rather than angry.

"I don't believe—"

"Tess has slipped off from a dance before. I'm just making sure she doesn't again."

"Did you ask her for a reason or just yell at her when she got home?" Lainie asked.

He stalked across the braided rug until he stood almost nose to nose with her. The intoxicating scent of him consumed her. The heat of his body poured over her.

''I knew the reason. Which is more than you know.''

Lainie held her anger in check, determined to be as cool-headed as he appeared. ''If you were having trouble, why didn't you write about it or call me sooner?''

''I thought you'd be here Christmas. I was going to discuss it with you then.''

His eyes probed hers. She saw a flicker of emotion she couldn't define before he became coolly controlled once more. She went to the window, biding time while she regained control of her own feelings.

''I invited Tess to visit me,'' she said. He had turned the tables. She was on the defensive now.

He gave a little snort that could have meant anything or nothing. ''Our dear sister couldn't tear herself away from her latest conquest. I had to do it for her.''

Lainie tried to understand the hidden meaning in this cryptic explanation. ''I've never been good at subtleties. Tell me straight out what you mean.''

''She went to a motel with a man,'' he said bluntly.

Lainie tried not to let the shock show. ''Oh.''

''I got there in time—''

''Poor Tess,'' Lainie said, imagining the girl's humiliation.

''Poor Tess, hell,'' Dev exploded. ''She led a love-struck cowboy around until he couldn't think straight. I had to fire a perfectly good hand because of her.''

"Did it ever occur to you that Tess might have been in love?" she asked, her voice quiet.

The anger seemed to leave him, and she saw the fatigue return. He shrugged. "She's too young to know what love is."

Lainie was silent for a minute. "You're handling Tess wrong."

"I suppose you think you can do better?"

Could she? What part had she ever played in Tess' life but that of a visitor? Perhaps it was time to throw off old memories and forge new bonds. She and Tess could really get to know each other. She could tell the younger girl that hearts do mend. But she wouldn't tell her who she had loved when she was sixteen and thought the world was wonderful. "Yes."

"Then do it." He walked to the door, stripping off his shirt as he went. "If you can bring yourself to stick around long enough." He gave her one long challenging glance and left the room.

Chapter Two

His boots thudded on the short flight of steps that led to the upper level of the house. In a moment, Lainie heard the shower come on. A vision of his body, lean and fit, bloomed in her mind. She wondered if a woman had ever shared the master suite with him. The thought hurt. It shouldn't, not after all this time. She had gotten over her girlish crush long ago, but it was still difficult for her to be near Dev. He was too dynamic, too complex. She had sometimes felt she wanted to strip away the layers and find the real person behind his silent scowl.

Restless, she picked up the magazine from the floor. It flopped open at an ad, one of those in which a man is talking on the phone to an unseen woman and making wonderfully romantic comments. She flung it on the coffee table.

Going to her room she brushed her hair and applied a bright lipstick as if it were a shield. Once Dev had looked at her with interest in his eyes, once he had almost kissed her in the stable.

Her lips softened at the memory—the close, intimate smell of the stable, the soft whickering of a mare to her newborn, the exchange of glances between them…the unconscious, instinctive moving together…

Then Charles had entered and the moment had flown with the cold blast of air from the door. She had been sent to the house, but she had stayed, ear pressed to the barn door, and had heard her stepfather speak to Dev, his voice harsh.

"Keep away from the girl," he had ordered. "I catch you looking at her like that again, I'll lay a strip of hide off you."

"If I'll let you," Dev had answered evenly, reminding his father he was a man, not a boy to be chastised with a belt.

"You get mixed up with her and you'll leave here."

"I'll leave now, if that's what you want," Dev had said, refusing to back down. He walked toward the door.

Lainie had run for the house then, her heart feeling as if it had outgrown her chest. The episode had been the final realization of her stepfather's feelings. She had hoped he would overcome his aversion toward her. Now, from his tone, she knew the truth. She also knew how much Dev loved the ranch. If anybody left, it should be her.

Anxious to be rid of the past, Lainie nearly ran over Dev when she left her room. He put out a hand to steady her. The sensation of his touch, coming on top of her memories, was like a torch to straw. She jerked away.

"Sorry, I wasn't thinking," she murmured.

"Or maybe you were thinking too much," he replied.

She stared at him, wondering if he knew her thoughts. No, of course not. Don't overreact, she issued her own warning to her unsteady nerves.

"Dinner," Agnes called.

Dev motioned Lainie down the short flight of steps.

She saw that the housekeeper had set the formal dining table for two. It seemed much too private. "Why don't we just eat at the kitchen table?"

"Dev's seen enough of my face," Agnes said, bringing in heaping bowls of fresh salad. She went out and returned with a covered basket of hot bread. "Yell when you're through."

Dev held out a chair, and Lainie had no choice but to take her seat. To protest further would have seemed infantile. He took the chair at the head of the table immediately to her left.

"We need to talk," he said.

"All right."

"After dinner. In the office."

He sighed, bringing her gaze to his face. His expression was impassive, but lines of fatigue still deepened the grooves at the sides of his mouth. She felt a tug of compassion. Charles had always expected so much from his only son.

"Has it been a difficult winter?" she asked, her voice soft with sympathy.

His glance flicked to hers. Their eyes connected and held, then he looked back at the table. "About the same."

"I saw the reports of the March blizzard. Did you lose any cattle?"

"Some."

She thought she detected impatience in his voice and dropped the line of questioning. Spearing a succulent leaf she ate quietly, answering his questions about her flight without elaboration. The second course of lamb stew was delicious, and they each complimented Agnes on it when she brought in bowls of sherbet.

"The coffee's in the office," she said. "I'll be leaving now. Would you put your bowls in the dishwasher when you finish and turn it on?"

"I'll take care of it," Dev promised.

He insisted that Lainie go to the office and relax while he took care of the dessert dishes. She took a seat at the end of the sofa and waited. His first words when he strode in surprised her.

"I owe you an apology."

He stopped on the other side of the coffee table.

His stance seemed relaxed, but his eyes were moody and a frown etched a line between his brows. She had never been able to figure out his opinion of her, not since those first months so many years ago when they had looked at each other with awareness in their eyes. After Charles had threatened to send him away because of her, Lainie had guarded herself around him. It was a habit of long-standing.

"For what?" she asked.

He gestured with one hand, a sweeping movement to indicate the events of the day. "Your arrival with no one to greet you, the argument between me and Tess, then my taking it out on you. My uncalled-for remark about your father."

She waved his apology aside. "It doesn't matter."

"Doesn't it?"

His eyes proved the depths of hers. She was puzzled. The anger she saw wasn't directed at her, she realized. Was he angry with himself for her poor reception? She didn't want him to feel that way. "No. I needed the time alone." At his raised brow she elaborated, "I was thinking of my mother. She loved this place."

"But you didn't, did you?"

The pointed question caught her off guard. She looked down at her fidgeting hands and clasped them together. "Of course I did. All kids love the idea of a ranch. I just...outgrew it. My life took a different turn."

"I see," he said with no inflection. She couldn't

tell how he interpreted her words. He sat in the easy chair across the table from her. "Pour me a cup, will you? Black, no sugar."

Her hands trembled as she poured coffee for each of them. They trembled more when she held out his cup to him. It was the one thing she hadn't mastered. She had learned to wear a bright smile around Charles, to pretend she wasn't aware of his dislike in order to spare her mother, but she had never been able to still the trembling of her hands when she was emotionally wrought.

Dev took a long swallow before speaking again. "Your father was right. You're beautiful without artifice."

She nearly dropped her cup at the compliment. "Thank you." She tried a smile and found she could hold it.

"Did you really think Tess' clothes were okay for a sixteen-year-old to wear in public?"

She answered hastily, grateful for the change of subject. "It wasn't as bad as the things some of the tourists wear. If you'd seen their getups, you'd realize Tess' outfit was quite sane by contrast."

"That's at a resort. This was a high school dance."

"It was okay. The idea was to be tacky. We used to have dances like that. Didn't you?"

He shrugged. "I don't remember any. I guess that makes me an old fogy who's no longer with it."

"No, it makes you an older brother who's prone

to be overprotective. Tess is a normal, rebellious teenager. A natural state of affairs, I think.''

He looked as though he would like to ask her a question. She waited expectantly. Apparently he changed his mind. ''I suppose. She has certainly been a trial for the past six months. Hormones?''

''Partly. Mostly just growing up and feeling her way.'' She sounded like a school counselor.

He placed the cup on the table and leaned his head against the high back of the chair. From beneath lowered lashes he observed her. ''What made you so wise, Lainie?''

A frisson drifted along her spine at his use of her name. She had to stop reacting to every nuance between them. ''I'm not, but I remember what it was like. Don't you?''

He stared at her for a long time. For a second, she thought she saw him soften. She thought she saw a return of that glance they had exchanged in the stable, of that irresistible drawing closer. What would have happened if they had completed the action and kissed?

''Yeah, I guess I do.'' His voice was the softest drawl, a growl, a purr. It touched places best left sleeping.

She looked away. ''I think you just need to be patient. Things will improve.'' She covered a yawn. It was past midnight back East.

''You're beat,'' he said. ''Go on up to bed. I forgot about the time difference. We can talk tomorrow.''

"What about?" She couldn't see that they really had anything to discuss. She had given him all the advice she could about Tess.

She rose. His eyes swept over her figure. She put her hands in her pockets as a tremor raced through her.

"About the future."

Tess' future? Their future? She shook her head to clear it. She really was tired if she was thinking along those lines. She headed for the door. "Good night, Dev."

"Good night. And welcome home, Lainie."

She was aware of a change in the atmosphere. Although the night was cooling rapidly, she thought the room seemed warmer. She hurried out.

At two o'clock she was pacing the floor. Where was Tess? The dance should have been over at 12:30. She was supposed to have been home at 1:30. The drive out from town was no more than fifty minutes. Was Dev awake?

At that moment she heard the *burrrrr* of tires on the bridge over the river. She breathed a sigh of relief. The couple had probably stopped for a hamburger before leaving town.

Lainie started to remove her robe and return to bed when she heard the sound of steps on the stairs. She raced across the room and threw open her door in time to see a masculine shape descend the stairs without turning on the lights. She rushed after him.

"Dev," she called urgently.

He stopped on the bottom step. "What are you doing up?"

"She's only a little late. Don't confront her now, not while you're angry," she advised. "Let me talk to her tomorrow."

He didn't move for a long minute, then he relented. "Okay. I'll leave it in your hands."

When he retraced his steps she saw that he wore jeans but no shirt. In the dark he was only an outline against the faint gleam of the porch light, but he looked broad and strong, as solid as the rocky land around them. The heart of the land, she thought, he was the living, beating heart of the land.

"Fine," she whispered when he paused in front of her. His intent regard made her nervous. She shivered.

"Go back to bed," he said in husky tones. "You're freezing."

"I'd forgotten how cold it gets at night in the high country."

He took her arm and ushered her to her door. "After a few weeks here, you'll remember." He released her and swiftly crossed the hall to his open door.

"I can only stay a couple of weeks," she said in surprise. She had agreed to visit for "a while." That didn't mean the whole summer, as he had implied. She wanted to set the record straight on that score. "Two weeks at the most."

"No." He closed his door.

She entered her room slowly, her mind furiously busy. He couldn't expect her to take weeks and weeks off. There were the store and her town house, plus a hundred other things. She removed her robe and climbed between the sheets. No one waited for her at her home. The store had an excellent manager. Actually, no one really needed her and hadn't in a long time. Until she had received the call from Dev.

Tess entered the kitchen at noon the next day still yawning sleepily. Lainie thought she looked much prettier without the bright makeup and with her hair falling in natural waves around her oval face.

"Good morning. How was the dance?" she asked, folding the newspaper and laying it aside. She hadn't awakened until nine o'clock herself. Agnes had said that Dev was out at the crack of dawn as usual. No wonder he looked tired.

"Okay. Everybody was there."

"Did it end at twelve-thirty? I seem to recall they rolled up the sidewalks at that time when I lived here."

Tess poured a glass of orange juice. "Yes." There was a slight hesitation. "I was a little late getting home. I'm glad Dev wasn't awake. He'd have probably grounded me for the rest of my life."

"Car trouble?" Lainie asked casually.

"Sort of. A couple of miles out of town I noticed the gas tank was on empty, so I made Robbie go back." Tess grinned. "He only had a dollar left. I pitched in another one. I figured that was enough to get me home and him back to his house. Can you imagine what Big Brother would have said if I had *walked* in about six this morning?'' She rolled her eyes dramatically.

Lainie laughed. ''That was astute of you to notice. And wise to insist on going back. It's a long drive to the ranch.''

Tess tossed her head in a pleased manner. She reminded Lainie of a young filly who had been praised for performing well. If she could only show Dev what a few words could do....

Agnes came in from the laundry room. ''You need to change your sheets today,'' she reminded Tess.

''I remember. I know it's clean-up-my-room day. And scrub the bathrooms.''

''I'll help,'' Lainie volunteered.

Tess wasn't bashful about accepting. ''Super. You do Dev's quarters. I'll do the rest.''

A little while later Lainie found herself vacuuming the carpet in the master suite. She had already stripped the bed and put on fresh sheets. The bathroom was sparkling, and sunshiny yellow towels hung on the racks.

The bedroom was pleasant, reflecting the colors her mother had loved—buttercup yellow accessories with off-white walls, a Persian rug of bright hues on the oak planking and pastoral paintings on the walls. A bright, loving room.

Tess stuck her head in the door. "Finished with the vacuum?"

"Just about." Lainie finished up the last swath. "Here."

"I'll do your room, too."

"Thanks."

Lainie smiled after Tess trundled off. Her younger sister wasn't terribly spoiled or selfish, nor did she have a mean streak. Lainie couldn't see any great problem with her.

She gathered the used sheets and towels. For a second she closed her eyes and breathed in the faint aroma of after-shave, soap and shampoo and the male scent that belonged to Dev.

Her body responded with sensual hunger, opening, blossoming, warming with desire. She wanted touching and tasting and...

Shaking her head as if to clear it of a bad dream, she counted the months...no, years...since she had last made love—two and a half, almost three years, she realized.

That was a long time to bury all the natural feelings of being a woman. Truthfully, she hadn't really thought about it until now. She didn't need a reawakening of useless passion.

Briskly, she carried her bundle to the laundry room, started the washer, and tossed it in. She checked the towels in the dryer. Dry. She folded them and returned them to the linen closet.

Tess bounded into the hall just as she finished

straightening the shelves. "You're just like Mom," Tess commented. "She always arranged things if they got out of order."

"You probably will, too, when you have a place of your own."

Tess wrinkled her nose in disbelief. "Well, I'm through. I've got to go to town. The juniors have to decorate the gym for the senior banquet tonight. We have to serve their dinner, too. I'm staying over with Hilary. Dev knows," she added at the question on Lainie's face.

"Have fun," Lainie called after her.

Tess answered on the run. "I will. Next year, I'll be a senior and get to be waited on and have off the whole last week of school, too. Yeaaaa!"

Lainie experienced an anxious moment when Tess dropped her overnight bag and it bounced off the wall and hit her feet. The teenager stumbled on the stairs but quickly recovered. Lainie unclenched her hands. Ah, to have that ability to rebound from the blows of life.

Lunch was served in the kitchen. Only she and Agnes were there. "Dev and Zed took sandwiches this morning. They're working away from the house," Agnes told her, setting out plates heaped with chicken salad and garden vegetables.

"What are they doing?"

"Putting up a gate in a box canyon. There's a wild stallion who's laid claim to the mares. Dev intends to catch him."

Lainie envisioned the wild horse being shot. "What will he do with it?"

"Tame it, most likely. Dev's good with animals."

After the meal Agnes went to her own house. Lainie roamed through the ranch house, then outside. The sun was high overhead. The air was warm. A hawk floated on a thermal above the ridge.

Standing on the back patio Lainie stared at the hawk. A wave of restlessness flooded her, so strong it was almost a pain. What she needed was some exercise. She was used to working all day.

She went to her room and found her swimsuit. It was one piece, printed in a diamond pattern of vivid pinks and navy blue. The legs were cut almost to her waist on the sides. The top part was relatively modest, the back nonexistent. She put it on. Draping a large towel over her shoulders, she slipped her feet into clogs and headed for the pool.

The pool, or swimming hole, was a natural depression in the rock at the base of a cliff. A hot spring bubbled out of the side of the cliff. Others, unseen, filled it from below. In the old days it had been called the "cowboy's bathtub."

Lainie tested it with a toe before dropping the towel and plunging in. It was as warm as she remembered. A natural hot tub.

Her rusty skills returned, and she swam the length of the pool over and over until she was tired. She spread the towel on the warm stone and rested in the sun. When she was dry she dabbed on sun block and lingered with her feet in the water.

The swim had been just what she needed to get her emotional equilibrium back. A few days here and she'd have all the kinks out. Cool, calm Lainie. That was how all her friends back East saw her. That was the way she was determined to be. No more getting sidetracked on the past. She would look upon this time as a vacation and use it to clear her mind. When she went back to Virginia Beach, it would be with a clean slate. She would start her life over.

Dev dropped the saddle across the rack and tossed the bridle on a hook. He pushed his hat off his forehead and wiped the sweat on his shirt sleeve. He and Zed had built the gate designed to trap the wild stallion that was causing havoc with the remuda. Damned mustang kept running off with his best mares.

The gate had been a good idea. They had managed to run the mares inside the box canyon, but the stallion was wily. The scent of man had spooked him and he had lit out for the high country. Maybe he wouldn't come back. Ha! Did any living male willingly give up an easy treat like a herd of tame fillies eager to be serviced?

His eyes darkened on that thought. His body stirred. Maybe he should spend a few more hours in the saddle. Would that make him numb enough not to respond? He doubted it. Ever since he had called

Lainie and she had promised to come out his blood
had raced at each thought, no matter how remote
from his own situation, on the natural order of
things—like mating and the rites of spring.

A cold shower under the garden hose and a soak
in the hot tub would take care of it, he decided. He
went to the mud room off the kitchen, grabbed a
towel from the cupboard, and headed out to the yard.

Behind the garden shed he stripped and washed in
the cold water from the hose, using a squirt bottle of
kitchen detergent for soap and shampoo. It smelled
of lemons. Finishing, he wrapped the towel around
his hips and tucked the edge in.

The flagstone walk was warm on the soles of his
feet. The lowering sun felt good on his shoulders. It
had been a hard day, getting the temporary gate up,
then chasing those damned horses all over kingdom
come.

Just as he turned the corner around a planting of
head-high shrubs, he heard a splash. He stopped, then
proceeded slowly.

He stopped again when he saw Lainie.

She was standing on the rock overhang that they
used as a diving board. Her hands were linked together over her head as she prepared to dive into the
clear pool. Her long black hair hung like a shimmering curtain halfway down her back.

Her body was slender, with long shapely legs that
made her look taller than the five and a half feet he
knew her to be. The cut of her bathing suit enhanced

the effect. Her breasts rose high and full beneath the diamond patterned material.

An ache manifested itself in the lower regions of his body as he went rigid with desire. He wanted to touch her the way he had yesterday when, unable to resist, he had caressed her soft lips. She'd be like that all over, he thought, soft and sweet....

She dived with one clean leap into the warm water. Breaking the surface again, she swam laps up and down the pool.

Her hair floated on the water like some magical seaweed, dark and enticing, luring a man into its silken strands until he was completely entangled... and happy to be there, even if he drowned.

Dev shook his head and beat down the flickers of heat that tried to burn all thought from his mind. Some primeval force in him called for action. He wanted to strip the towel away and join her. He wanted to do a hell of a lot more than that.

He wanted to slip the suit off her and admire her naked curves as they gleamed wetly in the sun. To touch her smooth skin. To carry her to the clumps of buffalo grass that formed a rough lawn to one side of the pool and make love to her until all the longing was burned out of his body.

Then maybe he could get on with his work and his life.

He clenched his fists and turned back toward the house. Debra, Lainie, Tess—what was it about those women, what had the daughters inherited from their mother that made men forget rational thinking when they were around?

He had been eighteen when his father had brought home his new wife. At first Dev had resented her, but no one could stay immune to Debra for long. She had had a keen sense of life. Her laughter had made every day sparkle. His father had been enslaved.

Dev thought of his mother, Grace. She had been a quiet woman with a hint of tragedy in her eyes even when she seemed happiest. It wasn't until his stepmother came to live with them and he heard the story of Charles and Debra's never-forgotten love that he had understood his mother's sadness. She knew she wasn't first in her husband's heart. Had never been. Could never be.

Dev gathered his clothes from the bench beside the shed. He headed for the kitchen door.

He'd never be trapped like that by a woman, he vowed. He'd never let himself be obsessed with a woman the way his father had been with Debra. It had been ridiculous the way a strong man like his father had kowtowed to Debra's every whim. Tearing out a storage room and installing a bath for her when she complained about having only one. Letting her redo the house. Moving rocks around in the yard for her.

Not that Debra had taken advantage, he added fairly. She hadn't been that kind of woman. In fact, he had come to love her. From the first she had dealt with him as one adult to another. Not many women were that wise. She had become his friend.

He entered the mud room and threw his dirty work clothes in the basket. His boots went in a corner. Agnes was checking a stewing hen when he stalked through the kitchen.

"Supper will be in the oven when you get through swimming," she said.

"I'm not going swimming," he snapped.

She closed the oven door and looked at him, naked except for the towel around his lean waist. "Your suit's in the third drawer of your bureau, if you feel you need one." Her grey eyes gleamed with silent mirth at this barb. He stalked off.

In his room he dressed in clean slacks and a knit shirt after shaving the day's stubble off his face. Unable to help himself, he went to the window and stared at the cliff and the bit of pool that he could see beyond the tall shrubs.

Lainie swam into view. She pulled herself out of the water and sat on a boulder to dry in the sun.

A groan forced its way out of him. The sun added a golden glow to her pale skin and cast diamond sparkles in her black hair. Once he had heard Zed singing *My Wild Irish Rose* in a wonderful tenor husky from several cups of Christmas cheer. Since that time he had associated the song with Lainie. He could see her now, standing next to the Christmas tree, a sprig of mistletoe in her hair, a sweet, wistful look in her eyes.

He had wanted to kiss her but couldn't. He had recently had a quarrel with his father over her when Charles had found them in the stable after one of the mares had foaled. He remembered the warm, salty scent of the birthing, the quiet sense of intimacy afterward. God, he wanted her with a passion that had seared his soul.

It was a good thing Charles had come in, he thought, his eyes hardening. He wouldn't be a slave to love or sex or whatever it was that drove men to sell themselves to the devil for just a taste of honeyed lips.

Honeyed lips? He already sounded as if he had lost half his wits. He glanced once more at Lainie before he 'went to the office to take care of some of the infernal paperwork a ranch produced. He'd never make a fool of himself over a woman, not in a million years.

Chapter Three

On Sunday, dressing for church, Lainie was more careful than she had ever been about putting on her makeup and choosing her outfit. She settled on a pink linen suit. An ecru blouse with a cascade of lace down the front lent an old-fashioned air to the ensemble. Sheer lace stockings made her feel utterly feminine.

Tess came in while Lainie was finishing her mascara. The girl's eyes were outlined in turquoise with a silver band over the top lid. She looked over Lainie's assortment of bottles and tubes.

"You have a lot of makeup," she commented.

"Umm-hmm," Lainie agreed. She surveyed her face critically. "I read that a thin cover of makeup is probably better for your skin than leaving it open to the pollution in the air these days."

"I guess it's better to have something on your face that you know than something that you don't, right?"

"Right." Lainie screwed the mascara wand into the tube and laid it down. She waited for Tess to continue.

The teenager looked as if she had something on her mind. She fidgeted with the strap of her purse, her teeth nibbling at her bottom lip.

When she didn't speak, Lainie turned to her. "That's a sweet dress. I can't decide if you look like a bride or a virgin about to be sacrificed to the gods."

Tess smiled and twirled around like a model, showing off her white lace dress and white stockings. Lainie was struck by how mature she looked. Her little sister was almost grown.

"I'll meet you downstairs," Tess said and left, her skirts swishing around her knees.

When Lainie went down Dev was already in the foyer. He was wearing a light gray suit. Unlike many ranchers who were uneasy without their boots and Stetsons, he seemed perfectly comfortable in black dress shoes and no hat. He looked up as she descended the steps.

"Tess will be here in a minute," she said, smiling and trying not to react to his presence.

He looked at her, then away, a frown settling between his brows. Although he had called and demanded that she come to the ranch, he evidently didn't like having her there. She stiffened her spine a bit. The opinion of Devlin Garrick didn't interest her in the least. She had long outgrown her need for male approval.

He walked to the door. ''What's keeping her?'' he asked, obviously impatient at having to wait for the womenfolk.

Lainie felt herself reacting defensively on Tess' behalf in spite of her resolve to remain calm. ''She'll be here any moment. Don't say anything about her makeup,'' she ordered sharply. ''Try to pick out something you like and compliment her on it.''

His glance narrowed as he took in every detail of her outfit, then settled on her face. He moved from one feature to another, lingering longest on her mouth. She wondered if she had smudged her lipstick.

''Does anything meet with your aproval?'' she asked coolly.

To her surprise, he smiled. It changed his whole aspect in an instant. Like a field of wild flowers, she thought. One day they weren't there, the next they were, as if a magic wand had been waved over the land. So it was with Dev. He was usually so serious, but when he smiled, the world seemed to bloom with the heady beauty of spring.

''Everything,'' he said in deepened tones. His jaw hardened and the smile disappeared. A brow lifted. ''You must know you're a beautiful woman. I've never yet met one who didn't.''

It was the second time he had called her beautiful, but the compliment was delivered with a barb this time. "Thanks," she said dryly. "Don't be cynical when you speak to Tess. She'll realize it and think you're being sarcastic."

The air hummed with tension as she returned his hard glance. He wasn't used to being told what to do. Perhaps she had overstepped her bounds, but she was determined that he would see the error of his ways regarding their younger sister before she left.

Heels clicked on the oak planking as Tess came out of her room and down the steps. She hesitated on the bottom stair as Dev looked her over. Lainie noticed that Tess had removed the gaudy layer of silver from her eyes and softened the line of color to a faint glow.

Dev smiled at his sister, then at Lainie. He held out an arm to each of them. "Now this," he said softly, "is how a man likes his women to look."

Lainie witnessed the heightening of color in Tess' cheeks. Her own felt warmer. His compliment had been just right. He glanced down at her, a question in his eyes. She nodded.

His gaze returned to Tess. "I like your hair like that. It looks soft and natural."

She tossed her head. "I thought I'd leave it down today," she said, uncertain how to take him.

Lainie sighed in relief. Dev and Tess were off to a good start, so her plan seemed to be working. The day was warm without being stifling. The breeze was gentle. All signs boded well.

Agnes was waiting for them in the car. Tess got

in the back. Dev opened the front door for Lainie. After she was seated she smiled over her shoulder at Agnes. When Dev started the engine she turned her eyes to the road. They looked like a family, she thought. Except she wasn't a Garrick. Once she had wanted so desperately to belong, to be a part of them....

There she went again, letting memories get the better of her. So much for her resolution to relax and start a new life with a clear head. What she needed was a fresh vision of the future, she decided. She would concentrate on that and on helping Dev learn to deal with Tess.

This decision made, she watched the countryside roll by until they reached the church where Garricks had worshiped for a hundred years. There she listened attentively to the preacher and stilled her thoughts. The morning passed swiftly.

"Lunch will be ready in five minutes," Agnes said when they arrived back at the house after the service. "Do you want to change first?" She looked at Dev.

He shook his head. "I'm not going to do any ranch work today. I thought we might swim this afternoon and go into town for a movie tonight." He looked at Lainie for an answer.

Tess, who'd been quiet on the ride home, seemed interested. "Say yes, Lainie," she coaxed. "This is the first time he's offered to go to a movie in ages. Usually I have to beg."

"Perhaps we should go," Lainie teased, "just so he'll remember how to act in polite society."

"Oh, I remember," he said. The corners of his mouth quirked into a droll grin.

Things were going well, she mused. She wouldn't have to stay more than a couple of weeks after all.

After the meal Agnes prepared to retire to her house. Lainie and Tess put the dishes in the washer, then went to change clothes.

Lainie slipped on her suit and walked to the pool. Dev was already there. He wore dark trunks made like running shorts. No white strip of flesh was visible at his waist or thighs when he climbed out of the water and dived from the ledge. Did he swim nude when no one was around? Don't even think it!

She forced her gaze to the far side of the pool. Prickly pears grew among the boulders. A clump of red-hot poker plant grew in a graceful circle nearby. Buffalo grass formed a green oasis amid the gravel and rocks.

She busied herself spreading a thin film of sun block over her face and shoulders. Her fingers trembled slightly. She wished she had better control when he was near. *If wishes were wings...*

Tess arrived in high-heeled clogs, sunglasses and a bright pink suit. She tossed the glasses on a boulder and kicked off her shoes. "Come on, Lainie. Last one in is a rubber duck."

Lainie dodged a splash as Tess took two steps and dived in, then swam the length of the narrow pool following in Dev's wake. Streamers of sunlight cut through the clear water, making long, slanting ribbons of light in the smooth water. The sky glowed like blue glass lit from behind. Lainie sighed and sought contentment. It came slowly.

Tess pulled herself from the pool and sat next to Lainie.

"Pink is your color," Lainie complimented. "It looks perfect with your honey-brown hair and eyes."

"Thanks." Tess studied Lainie's outfit. "That's a new suit, isn't it? It looks great on you, but it's cut higher than those things you used to wear."

"I know," Lainie said. "The stores don't stock anything but French-style these days. If they get any higher, we'll have to start wearing something under them for modesty."

"I wish my legs were as long and slender as yours."

"You're still growing," Lainie assured her. "I think we both have Mom's general shape."

"I agree," a male voice chimed in. Dev had stopped swimming and was treading water in front of them.

Water clumped his eyelashes. It ran off his hair onto his shoulders. She noticed how hard and fit he looked. A shiver invaded her middle, and she looped her arms across her stomach in defense.

"Aren't you coming in?" he asked.

"Maybe. In a minute," she added when his eyes

took on a dangerous gleam. "I want to enjoy the sun."

Agnes yelled out the back door. "Tess, telephone."

"That must be Hilary," she said and dashed away.

Lainie didn't want to be alone with Dev. She couldn't think of anything to say. Why was she being so ridiculous these days?

"Remember the time we held a contest to see who could bring up a stone from the deepest part?" he asked. He felt briefly nostalgic for days that used to be before he had so much work and responsibility filling his life.

He remembered the first time he had seen Lainie in the pool. She had been dressed in a two-piece bathing suit of some shiny, stretchy material that had fitted her lithe body like a gossamer web. That had been years ago, but nothing had changed. She looked just as attractive now as then, and he reacted just as strongly.

It was a good thing he was still in the water. His physical reactions to her were swift and predictable. Any time she was near his body was aroused. It was damned embarrassing for a thirty-five-year-old man. His face hardened.

Lainie's contentment ebbed upon seeing the frown return to Dev's face. For a moment he had looked young again. She wondered what he had been thinking.

"You've kept the landscaping the way Mother

planted it,'' she finally said when the silence stretched uncomfortably between them.

He looked around. ''Debra understood living things. Where they would grow, where they wouldn't.''

Once, after a bitter quarrel with his father about introducing a new breed into the cattle herd, he had decided to leave. Debra had stopped him.

''Your home is here,'' she had said. ''The city would change you, if you moved away. Stay.''

He had realized she was right when he had cooled down. He had later broached the subject again and his father had been receptive to the idea. Debra's doing? he had wondered. Probably.

''Do you miss them?'' Lainie asked. ''Your father and mother?''

''Sometimes. Debra, too. Sometimes I miss you more.''

Lainie was shaken by his confession. ''Why?'' she finally asked. Her equilibrium was slipping again.

''Once we were young together. We did things together—''

Was she imagining the loneliness in his eyes? ''I probably drove you crazy with all my questions. Most likely, you wanted to strangle me, or whatever brothers do to obnoxious sisters.'' She kept her voice light.

''You're not my sister,'' he said fiercely. ''I never thought of you like that. It was too late when we met. I was already a man, and you were...''

"Sixteen going on thirty," she supplied when he hesitated. "Smart-alecky."

He shook his head. "Never that, Lainie." He swam to the end of the pool and climbed out. The next thing she knew he was gone.

An ache settled in her heart. The familiar tremor attacked her hands. Absently, she unscrewed the cap of the sun lotion and smeared more on her face and arms.

Had he known how she felt about him? She had tried so hard to hide it, especially after she discovered her stepfather's antagonism toward her.

Life could be so confusing. She had always sympathized with Charles. It still seemed romantic and heartbreaking to love someone for years and years, knowing it was hopeless. But things had worked out for Charles and Debra. They had had many happy years together. And she had been content with her life.

Until now.

Lainie retired to her room and read until it was time for dinner. Then she went to the kitchen to prepare sandwiches. Tess came in and helped. When the meal was ready Lainie called Dev. They ate quickly and prepared for the long drive into town. Tess, dressed in jeans and a Western shirt, jumped in back. Lainie sat in front with Dev.

The movie was just starting when they arrived and found seats. Tess' friend had saved one for her. Dev and Lainie took two nearer the back. He bought a bucket of popcorn to share with her.

It was intimate, dipping into the same carton, their hands occasionally brushing, then munching on the buttery treat. Lainie couldn't remember when she had last been to a movie. The same length of time since she had last made love, she mused, then was appalled at herself.

This is his fault, she decided. The warmth of his shoulder near hers, the touching and sharing, all stirred up feelings long buried. She didn't want to resurrect them.

"What's wrong? Aren't you enjoying the show?" Dev leaned close to ask. He sounded genuinely concerned.

The scent of his after-shave washed over her. Lainie licked her fingers and shook her head. "I mean, yes, I am enjoying it. Very much." She fastened her eyes on the screen and refused to look at her companion. He was much too close there in the dark.

At last the movie was over. Dev politely took her arm and forged a path for them through the crowd. She started to climb in the back seat of the station wagon, but Dev was there before her, opening the front door. Tess was still talking to her friend several feet away.

"Have I offended you?" he asked. He jiggled the car keys in his free hand impatiently.

"No, of course not. I just thought Tess might like to ride in front during the ride home."

"Get in," he said and heaved an exaggerated sigh. "Come on, Tess." He opened the back door for her after Lainie was inside.

Except for a few desultory remarks about the movie they were quiet on the way home. The fifty-minute drive seemed to take forever. When they arrived she sighed in relief.

Dev went directly to the study after she refused a nightcap with him. She and Tess went upstairs.

"Lainie?" Tess said.

"Yes?"

"Oh, nothing."

Lainie paused at her bedroom door. "Do you want to come in and talk?" she invited.

Tess shook her head. "You're probably tired. I'll catch you another time."

Lainie said good night and closed her door. Tess had looked unhappy and troubled. She considered pressing for a discussion, but perhaps it was better to let the younger girl come to her.

It had been an unsettling day in many ways. She was used to going about her life alone. It wouldn't do to depend on the company of Dev and Tess. She had always held a peculiar position in the household, neither sheep nor wolf. She didn't exactly belong, but she wasn't exactly an outsider. At any rate, she wouldn't be here long enough to become used to companionship.

A slight smile touched her lips at the analogy. When Dev had looked at her in the movie tonight, she had seen something hot and hungry flash into his eyes. For a second his glance had been that of a predator. No, that was crazy. How could she read his thoughts in the flickering light of the theater when she couldn't in broad daylight?

But once, a part of her insisted, he had looked at her that way, as if he would give his soul for her. She had wanted him the same way.

On Friday she rode into town with Agnes and looked around while the housekeeper bought groceries. While she was exploring, she discovered a gift and antique shop and couldn't resist going in to see what the store stocked and how it was displayed.

The first thing she saw was dust. That would never do. Every piece of merchandise in her store was dusted every day. Also, the displays were changed regularly, not only in the windows, but on the floor, in order to give customers fresh ideas on how to use the items. From the faded red of the velvet in the window, she suspected it hadn't been changed in years.

"Oh, hello. Just look around all you please. I'll be in the back if you need me."

Lainie glanced around in time to see a curly gray head pop out of sight around a door. She walked to the back of the store. The woman who had spoken was bending over a crate, a crowbar in her hand. She was clumsily using the tool to pry off the lid.

"Here, let me help," Lainie volunteered.

She took the crowbar and wedged it expertly under one corner of the crate. With a steady pressure she raised the lid a quarter inch. She moved down the side, prying the nails loose as she went. In a couple of minutes she had worked around the box, loosening the top evenly on all sides. It was a simple matter to ease it the rest of the way off without splintering the wood.

"That was well done." The woman beamed at her. "Since my son moved to Phoenix, I've had a terrible time with things like that. I'm Dora Wynne." She held out her hand.

Lainie shook her hand. "Lainie Alder."

"You look familiar." Dora studied her with open curiosity. "I know. I saw you with the Garrick bunch at church last Sunday."

"Yes, my mother was—"

"Married to Charles Garrick. I remember now. You must be the daughter who lives back East. Don't you have a shop?"

Lainie nodded.

"Your husband passed away a while ago, didn't he? At least you know how to open a box," she went on.

Lainie realized she didn't have to answer the questions. She listened as Dora gave a matter-of-fact account of her problems since her son had moved to the city.

"Well, I can't blame him. Got a good job, he did. With the state. He said I ought to come on down. His wife—she's a good girl, local and all—found a retirement complex she thinks I'd like. They want me nearer to them and the grandchildren."

As she talked she unpacked figurines and handed them to Lainie. Lainie lined them up on a counter and wondered why Dora would buy a dozen identical shepherdesses. She doubted that a town this size would have a market for them.

"I have to admit I miss the little scamps. There's a picture somewhere." Dora shoved the wrapping paper into the crate and reached for a two-photo frame standing on the shelf behind the figurines. She handed the frame to Lainie.

The pictures were of two tow-headed boys, one about three, the other five or six. They smiled shyly into the camera with identical dimples in their right cheeks. Lainie's heart contracted. She had wanted children, but they had put it off too long.

"They look delightful," she said sincerely.

Dora took the frame and glanced at the boys affectionately. She placed it on the shelf and dusted her hands briskly. "Would you keep an eye on things? I'll run next door and get us a cup of coffee. You take anything in yours?"

"No, just black, please."

Lainie had coffee with Dora and spent a pleasant

morning talking shop while she waited for Agnes. Three customers came in; Dora showed them her new stock. Two of them bought the porcelain figures.

"They'll turn up at the next church bazaar," Dora announced cheerfully after the women left. "Say, you ever think of opening a shop here? Be close to your family."

"No, I—"

"Why, that'd be just the thing. Solve my problem and yours, too, wouldn't it?"

"Problem?"

"A person like yourself, used to being busy," Dora explained. "You'd need something to do, something of your own, to handle, I 'spect. Of course, if you took over the ranch books, that'd probably keep you occupied."

"I'm not coming back here to live," Lainie quickly put in. She wanted to squelch any rumors along those lines right off.

Dora gave her a puzzled glance. "But you don't have any family back East, do you?"

"My shop—"

"Sell it," Dora advised with a grin. "Buy this place. Cheap," she added as the door opened and Dev stuck his head in.

"Ready to go?" he asked. "Agnes went ahead. I said I'd pick you up. Hello, Dora, what are you trying to sell Lainie?" His smile was full of good-natured teasing.

If only he would be like this every day, Lainie

thought, instead of so stern and frowning most of the time.

"I'm trying to sell your sister the shop. No use in her living off by herself when she's got family out here."

"My stepsister," he corrected. He gave Lainie a particularly penetrating look before turning his smile on Dora again.

"I'd give her a really good deal," Dora continued, sensing a possible ally in him. "I could stick around and help her get started."

"Who owns the building?" Dev asked.

"I do. I'd be willing to sell it or lease it with the store."

"What do you think?" he asked Lainie.

Lainie stared at Dev dumbfounded. As if a person could make a decision of such importance just like that! "I have a place in Virginia Beach."

"She'll think about it," he told Dora.

"Good. Say, I've been trying to get some help in here. Would Tess want a summer job?"

Dev pushed his hat back and considered. "I usu-ally keep her pretty busy at the ranch." He glanced at Lainie. "What's your opinion? A job in town, earning her own money…?" His voice trailed into a question.

"Why don't you let her decide?" Lainie suggested firmly. "It was lovely talking to you, Dora."

"Drop by again. Soon."

"Thank you. I will."

Dev escorted Lainie to his pickup and held the door for her while she made the giant step into the cab. Several bags of ranch supplies were in the back.

"Why don't you buy Dora's place?" he asked after putting the truck in gear and easing into the busy flow of Friday traffic.

"What?"

"I said, why don't—"

"I heard what you said," she snapped.

"Well?"

"The idea is ridiculous."

"Why?"

"Because I have enough to do at the store I already have. I need to find some items for the fall stock. I should be in Europe now. We have two new people starting after the summer students leave. I need to train them. There are a hundred other things to do. That's why," she finished in a rush as if she needed to get her reasons laid out in a row for inspection.

His face had lost its teasing look. His jaw took on the line of masculine determination she had seen when he faced his father that time in the stable.

"Is it money?" he asked, giving her the harsh flick of his gaze before he turned onto the country road that would take them to the ranch. "Your share is still in the bank. It's a healthy balance by now."

"That's not my money," she said stiffly.

"A third of everything the ranch makes is yours,"

he reminded her. He spoke in a low tone, but his voice held a rough edge.

For some reason that totally escaped her, Charles had left a third of the income from all his holdings to her. The will had been very specific: Dev held title to the land; the three children, Dev, Lainie and Tess, were to share the net income for life. She had refused to take it, had even had her attorney write a letter to that effect. Dev continued to put the money in a bank account in her name. She received a statement every year and had to include the income and interest on her tax forms. The situation was very aggravating.

"I don't know why your father did that," she admitted. "You must resent it—"

"No, I don't," he said before she could finish.

"Well, I don't need it. I'm quite well-off." She tilted her chin at an angle. She was actually wealthy and didn't need to work at all. Her husband had been a lawyer and an astute investor.

They passed the turnoff to Sycamore Canyon. Water was running in the creek. Summer could be a dangerous time in this arid land with its sudden thunderstorms that filled the washes. Flash floods claimed lives every year. The storms of longing she experienced around Dev were dangerous, too. She'd better watch it, or her common sense would be swept away.

A mile farther on, Dev turned right. A sign read: Garrick Canyon Ranch Road. Private Property.

"You know why my father left you the money,"

he said as if there had been no lapse in the conversation.

She said nothing.

"He felt guilty."

"G-guilty?" She cleared her throat, angry with herself for the break in her voice. It gave away more than she wanted to disclose.

"It was his way of atoning for his cruelty to you."

Lainie clasped her hands over her purse strap. "Charles was always nice to me. He was never cruel."

"He couldn't stand the sight of you." Dev geared down to take a rough patch in the road. His face was set in a hard expression that she found impossible to read. "You reminded him too much of Robert, the man who married Debra."

"Charles married your mother right after that," Lainie reminded him, "and had you two years before I was born."

Dev gave a harsh chuckle. "I never said his attitude was reasonable. He was jealous of your father. It affected his treatment of you. He wanted to make that up to you. We all knew why you left."

"I went for the education. Charles was very generous about that." She found it was important to her that Dev not think less of his father for being human.

"And we all pretended to believe your reasons; otherwise, their marriage would have ended in divorce. My father couldn't bear to lose Debra again.

I think he would have died." He ended on a quiet note that sent a shiver up her spine.

"Yes," she agreed huskily. "They loved each other very much."

"All their lives. Even when they were married to other people."

Lainie glanced at him but could tell nothing from his tone or his expression. Had he known of his father's love for Debra during the years of marriage to Dev's mother? That marriage had lasted almost sixteen years before Grace had gotten flu, then pneumonia.

"Anyway, the money's yours," he finished.

"No. I don't need it. I won't take it."

"Then it'll stay in the bank." He bit off the statement and clamped his mouth shut as if he withheld a torrent of furious words demanding to be spoken.

"Fine. It's been there for two years. It can stay there forever," she said. "Or maybe I'll give it away. I'm sure there are many charities that would be glad of the extra funds."

She couldn't believe how mulish she sounded. This was not the way to win friends or influence people, which was what she really wanted to do. Be sensible, she reminded her temper.

She stole a glance at him from the corner of her eye. His eyes intercepted hers. She saw it again, a fleeting look of hunger that made her pulse beat wildly in every vital point of her body.

The passion she felt for him, which had been sleeping, was now wide-awake.

Chapter Four

"School's out, school's out, teacher's let the fools out," Tess sang when she entered the kitchen the next morning.

"Readin' an' writin' an' 'rithmatic," Lainie chimed in, setting her coffee cup down.

They harmonized on the next line, "Taught to the tune of a hick'ry stick."

Tess sighed as if she were already nostalgic for the good old days. "Can you believe it? One more year to go. I'm going to be a senior, come fall." Her eyes narrowed in determination. "Then maybe some people will take me seriously."

Agnes spoke up from the sink where she was trimming a roast. "Like your brother or a lonesome cowboy we both know?"

Color leaped into Tess' face. "Maybe," she mumbled. She poured milk on her cereal and joined Lainie at the table. Her eyes seemed sad all at once, and Lainie felt a pang of sympathy. The "ups" were so high and the "downs" so low at that age.

"Has Dev spoken to you about the job at Dora Wynne's store?" Lainie asked, changing the subject.

Tess glanced up, the melancholy replaced by a spark of interest. "What job?"

Had he forgotten or was he not going to let Tess take the position? Feeling she had probably stuck her foot in her mouth Lainie continued, "She asked about you yesterday and wondered if you'd be willing to help out. It most likely pays minimum wage."

Tess shook her head, her expression going flat. "Big Brother won't let me. I have to help take care of the horses and garden in the summer."

"I'll talk to him," Lainie declared. A hint of temper gleamed in her eyes. Together she and Tess cleaned the upstairs rooms, dividing the labor as they had before.

Lainie didn't see Dev until late that afternoon when he came to the house for a tractor part. He was getting the equipment ready to cut hay for winter feed. Seeing him in the paddock next to the tool shed, she hurried outside.

"I spoke to Tess about the job in the gift store," she said without preamble when she approached him.

He stopped looking through a can of nuts and bolts and gazed at her. His hat brim was pulled low over his forehead, shading his eyes. She wanted to push it up so she could see every flicker of thought in them.

"How'd she take it?" he asked, going back to his task.

"I think she'd like to try. It'd be good for her," she added, sounding defensive although she wanted to be matter-of-fact.

"Give her a little town polish?" he suggested without looking up. He was back to being cynical.

Lainie felt like knocking the can out of his hands, except she could see herself down on all fours for hours picking up every one of the blasted things. "She hardly needs it. She's very poised for a sixteen-year-old." Lainie remembered that Tess had a birthday coming up. "She'll be seventeen in less than a month. I'd like to give her a car of her own," she said on impulse.

That grabbed his attention. His clear-as-cider eyes stared into hers. Then she saw them move from her face to her body, all the way down to her feet and back up to her eyes. "Why do I get the feeling we're having a fight, only I don't know the subject of it?" he questioned after a lengthy pause.

"We're not fighting," she protested, then added, "But why haven't you told her about the job offer?"

"I'm still thinking about it." He scowled at her, but Lainie wasn't intimidated. Dev might be tough, but he wasn't mean.

"I'm going to tell her to stop by and talk to Dora," Lainie decided on the spot. If she were going to play a part in Tess' life, she might as well start now.

He straightened to his full height, pushed his hat up on his forehead and rocked back on his heels. His lashes dropped over his eyes so Lainie could see they were only a glitter. "If you'd already decided she could try it, then why are you bothering me about it?"

"It seemed the polite thing to do. I won't in the future." She spun on the ball of her foot.

He caught her arm before she could leave. "Wait," he said, his frown nicking a deeper crease in the middle of his forehead. "We used to get along better than this. What's wrong, Lainie?"

"Nothing." She squirmed out of his grip.

"You're as nervy as a june bug at a convention of frogs." His short laugh sounded forced.

"Don't be ridiculous."

He caught her by the shoulders. "I'm not. I know we weren't very welcoming when you arrived last week, but surely you're over that by now. You were never one to carry a grudge."

Lainie was aware of how close he was, his mouth only inches from hers as he gazed down at her with a puzzled expression.

He continued in a softer tone, "When Alice Combs spilled a soda on you at the church social that time because she was jealous of all the boys hanging around you, you didn't even get mad."

"It was an accident—"

"No, it wasn't, and you knew it. But you were nice to her for the rest of the time you were here. Which wasn't long," he added.

His hands released their grip and stroked along her upper arms. The sensation this produced was anything but soothing. Lainie clenched her hands and pressed her fists against his shirt. The warmth of his chest immediately transmitted itself to her.

"Why didn't you spend the summers with us? You were always off on one expedition or another, digging for artifacts, teaching Indian children to read, or a thousand other things…until you married. Was it because of my father?"

"Of course not. I was interested in archeology at the time. There was this cute guy in my class I had a crush on." She mentally crossed her fingers at this string of lies.

His lips thinned with disgust. He obviously didn't believe her. "Tell the truth. It doesn't matter now, but tell me anyway," he demanded in a slightly hoarse voice.

His gaze was so compelling that she felt her resolve melting. She wanted to tell him about everything, the loneliness and the times she cried herself to sleep when she returned to the boarding school or college dorm, the achy yearning that attacked whenever he was near, how it scared her to want somebody so. *He* was the reason she hadn't returned. Not because she wanted to spare her mother's or Charles' feelings, but because she couldn't handle what she had felt for him. She still couldn't.

"Let me go, Dev," she whispered.

"Tell me," he said.

Taking her courage in hand she returned his stare. "Things were…too difficult for me at that age." She tried to smile. "You know how seriously young people take life."

He sighed and released her. His gaze swept across the valley to the far ridge of hills. "Don't we all?" he said cryptically. "Tell Tess to take the job if she wants to. I'll help Agnes with the garden."

Lainie nodded and returned to the house. When Tess heard the news she seemed delighted. She rushed upstairs to dress and go into town to see Dora before the woman changed her mind. Lainie had to smile. At that age she had been impatient, too.

She went to her room and was drawn to the window. Dev had already left for the hay field where the combine waited. She changed to her suit and swam for a while. Later she helped Agnes gather greens from the garden. When Tess returned she informed them that she started work on Monday.

Dev came to the house at six, bathed, changed and left after speaking to Agnes. The three women ate alone, then Lainie and Tess watched TV until eleven. An hour later Dev arrived home and Lainie at last went to sleep.

Lainie wasn't sure what had awakened her. She glanced at the bedside clock, then pulled the covers over her shoulders. The desert air was chilly. She yawned and closed her eyes again. A distinct thumping brought her upright. She went to the window.

The moon was low and full and silver bright—a howling moon Charles used to call it. Its light cast a pewter glaze over the land. She saw Dev walk out of the shadows of the house and head for the stable.

That's where the thumping had come from. She heard it again. Quickly she threw off her gown and ran to the closet. She grabbed her jeans, put them on, then found her favorite oversize cotton sweater. After tugging it over her head, she slipped on her loafers and headed downstairs.

She felt like a spirit as she flitted across the driveway to the stable. She paused outside the door and listened. All she heard was a murmur of sound from within. Cautiously she opened the door. It creaked on its hinges, and she jumped violently.

"Come on in and shut the door," Dev ordered. "You're letting in cold air."

She did as directed. It took her a few minutes to get accustomed to the dim light in the interior, which was illuminated only by the moonlight that shone through the stable's mullioned windows. When her eyes had adjusted, she went to the stall where Dev stood stroking a young stallion's neck.

"Easy, boy," he was saying, "what's the problem, huh? Something scare you? There now, it's okay."

The stallion threw its head up when Lainie came over.

"Hey, it's just Lainie. She wouldn't hurt you. She's a nice lady. Yeah, very nice."

He went on speaking in a low croon until Lainie was also under his spell. She laid her arms on the top of the stall. Her chin rested on her crossed hands as she watched Dev calm the horse. The stable was warm...quiet...she felt so sleepy.

"Good boy. Easy does it. Go back to sleep. It's two o'clock in the morning. Good boy," Dev was saying.

Lainie yawned and slumped against the planks. He had the most wonderful voice...deep...mellow... husky.

Then the stallion let out a scream so loud and startling that she screamed, too. The challenge was immediately answered from outside the stable.

"That damned Appaloosa," Dev cursed.

The young stallion trumpeted again and kicked at the wooden box that confined him. Dev ran to the back door that led into the paddock. Lainie followed him outside.

The wild stallion was a thing of exquisite beauty. He stood on the ridge behind the house, his legs planted in a belligerent stance. His coat shone like old silver, dappled with patches of black on his chest and haunches.

"I'll kill him if he's taken more of my mares," Dev muttered.

Lainie caught his arm when he started toward the house. "No, don't. I won't let you hurt him." She threw both arms around his chest and clung, forcing him to take the bulk of her weight.

"Dammit, Lainie," he growled in her ear. His hard hands encircled her waist.

They glared at each other, their faces no more than four inches apart, frozen like statues in the moonlight. She didn't know how much time passed, or when the mood changed. But it did.

His hands tightened, but instead of pushing her away, he brought her closer, until every line of her body was molded against his. She experienced his body first as a sensation of strength, then as an increasing warmth.

"Lainie," he murmured.

She shivered when his breath touched her lips. Now, she thought. Now, at last we'll have the kiss we didn't get to share all those years ago.

The sound of splintering wood broke the spell.

He said an expletive she'd never heard him use and left her. Before he could reach the door the young stallion charged out, his head high, mane and tail flying. He and the Appaloosa thundered their furious challenges into the night, shattering its crystal perfection.

"Don't let him jump the fence," Dev shouted. "Keep him circling, else they'll kill each other. I may do it for them," he added as he threw up his arms, causing the stallion to break stride and turn aside.

Lainie clapped her hands together and ran behind him, but not too close. The horse circled the railed paddock in confusion.

"Let's head him for the door," Dev directed.

She stood to one side while he shooed the stallion toward the door, then she moved forward, waving her arms to each side to block a charge. Frustrated, the stallion turned and ran into the stable. She and Dev entered behind him. While she dropped the bar across the door, Dev tried to herd the excited horse into another stall, one without a broken latch.

Just when he succeeded the stallion kicked out with its powerful hind legs, catching Dev on his thigh with one and snarling a coil of metal cable on a post hook with the other. The cable caught on a hoof, and the stallion went down with a "hhufff" of surprise.

Lainie realized both man and beast were injured. The horse got to its feet, but it held a back hoof off the ground. Dev was cursing a streak as he gripped his bruised thigh. She heard him say something about making glue out of the... The rest of the statement was lost between gritted teeth.

"Here, let me help you sit down," she offered, taking his arm and putting it about her neck.

"See about the damned horse," he said. He hobbled to a bale of straw and sat on it, his leg straight out in front of him.

Lainie hung the coils of twisted cable on the hook

and shooed the trembling stallion completely into the stall. She went to the tack room where she knew liniment was kept. She spied an electric lantern on the windowsill and flicked it on. An old refrigerator supplied ice for cold compresses. She found an ace bandage and tucked it into her pocket, the liniment into another. Picking up the compresses and the lantern, she returned to the stable.

"Take your pants off," she ordered Dev. "I have ice for the swelling." She laid the folded towel next to him, hung the lantern on a post and went into the stall. "Easy now, boy, easy."

"Get the hell out of there. Are you trying to get yourself killed?" he demanded. He emitted a low groan when he tried to stand and fell back on the straw.

"Use that compress," she said, giving him a stern look over her shoulder.

Carefully, she examined the animal's injured hock, then wrapped the ice pack around it. The ace bandage kept it in place. She soaked the whole bundle with liniment before going to Dev.

He had the other ice pack resting on his bare leg. She knelt beside him. "Let me see."

"It's okay," he growled.

"Stop being a bear," she snapped. "I'm going to look at your leg whether you want me to or not."

Reluctantly he moved his hand. He grabbed his jeans and laid them modestly over his briefs. Lainie rolled her eyes, then lifted the towel. The injury was on the outside of his thigh, a glancing blow, fortunately, else the bone would have probably been broken. She felt it gingerly. No sharp edges or rough patches under the skin, just the red imprint where the hoof had struck.

"You'll have a nice bruise, but I think it's okay. We can go in and have it checked and X-rayed in the morning."

"I don't need a doctor," he said. "Go on back to bed."

"You are the worst patient. I feel like bonking you one myself." She eyed him as if deciding on the action.

"Try it," he challenged.

"No, you'd sit on me and pound my head into the dirt." She smiled to lighten the situation. She was very much aware of the lateness of the hour and the fact that they were alone.

"I'd pound something," he promised in an undertone.

She replaced the ice pack over the swelling and poured the liniment over the whole thing. Then she sat back on her heels and waited for him to try and stand.

Other than the whuffle of the stallion, it was eerily silent. The hair crept up on the back of her neck. "Can you make it to the house now?" She had to get out of there.

"You go ahead."

"I'm not leaving you."

"Go on. I'm all right."

She decided he must be hurt worse than he was letting on. "Put your arm around my neck and lean on me."

She'd probably melt when he touched her, she thought ruefully. In spite of this dire threat she decided she'd have to help him to the house. She lifted his hand, dislodging the jeans across his lap. They slithered to the floor.

She saw the reason for his reluctance to move. A flush of heat swarmed out of someplace in her abdomen and buzzed off to every point in her body. She was suddenly on fire, as aroused as he obviously was.

Fighting for control she managed a light laugh. "Well," she said, "your injury can't be too painful if you're thinking along those lines."

"Very funny," he said.

She returned his exasperated glare with more composure than she felt. The air seemed to sizzle with unspoken needs. His expression changed, and he seemed a gentler, softer man compared to the harsh one of a moment ago.

"Get out of here, Lainie," he ordered in a husky voice.

She couldn't move. Time ceased to have meaning to her.

He cursed under his breath, but his hands reached for her, dragging her into the circle of his arms.

"Dev," she whispered, afraid the moment would be snatched away, yet uncertain if she should take it.

"Don't talk. Not now. It's too late."

He lifted his hands to cup her head and run his fingers into her hair. In his eyes was every dream she had ever had of them. She should say something to prevent the kiss she knew was coming. No words came to her.

Her lips parted as he bent to her.

The kiss didn't come. Instead he paused with his lips no more than an inch from hers. "If you knew how often I've thought of this moment. To take it almost seems sacrilege."

"Perhaps we'll make the gods angry," she said, understanding his doubts.

He closed the space between them. His lips brushed across hers, making her skin burn and the ache inside grow. He caressed her again, moving the other way across her mouth. It was the lightest of touches, yet she felt it clear to her soul.

Feeling she was about to lose her balance, she laid her hands on his thighs. Powerful muscles flexed under her palms.

"Yes," he murmured, his eyes going dark as he lifted his head. "All my life you've been taboo to me. I'm almost afraid to touch you now."

She thought she would die if he didn't. The thought must have shown on her face.

A slight smile touched his lips and was gone. "But I have to," he whispered hoarsely. "I may burn in hell, but anything has to be better than the fire that tortures me now.''

"I know."

"Do you?"

They kissed.

Now time raced faster than their beating hearts as the seconds and minutes sped past just when she wanted them to tick slowly. She wanted to hold this moment so that she could store every detail of how his lips felt on hers.

She arched upward, seeking the strength of his body to still the dizziness in her. His legs moved, opened to receive her, and she was held in the strong embrace of his thighs as well as his arms. Sensations were hitting her from so many different sources she couldn't distinguish them all. But there, in the tight, intimate bonding of their bodies, she felt the demanding force of his male need and knew an answering need in herself.

The kiss deepened as his tongue sought the honeyed boundaries within her mouth. He thrust against her tongue, forcing her to retreat, then coaxed her into reciprocating, so that a mutual fire burned between them.

Oh, yes, this is bliss, she thought, and knew she had never felt it before.

She raised her arms and clasped them around his neck. Her hands splayed over his shoulders, then flowed along the contours of his back. She felt his muscles bunch beneath his shirt as he brought her even closer to his fiery heat. He slid his hands down her back to cup her buttocks and slowly move her from side to side.

A gasp was torn from her when he released her mouth and left hot, sweet kisses along her neck. He held her in a spell as he dipped lower to the collar of her sweater and touched each pulse point along her throat.

"Do you remember that other time?" he asked. "It was dark then, too, and the world seemed to disappear."

"There were just the two of us," she murmured. "And the mare and foal. Yes, I remember."

"Have you ever wished for those days to come back? Have you ever wanted to live them again, only this time you'd do things differently?" His hands became still as he spoke.

Images flitted through her mind: she and Dev riding like demons over the range, racing each other; she saw them swimming in the pool, challenging each other to touch the bottom; she saw them cleaning the stables…she and Dev…together.

She recalled other times that weren't so pleasant, such as the time she had heard Charles and her mother quarreling about her. Her mother had threatened to leave if he couldn't control his feelings toward Lainie.

"The past was not her fault. It was none of her doing, and I will not have her hurt because you're jealous of another man. I was married to Robert. We had a child. Those are the facts.''

''You'd leave me?'' Charles had demanded, incredulous and furious.

''Yes,'' her mother had replied. ''As much as I love you, I'd still leave. I won't have Lainie hurt.''

Lainie closed her eyes. For a second the ghost of Charles Garrick hovered in the shadows above her head, then she forgot him and all the reasons she shouldn't be in Dev's arms. She had waited too long for the moment to come to give it up.

Dev resumed his restless search. His hands moved up her back, slipping beneath the thick knit of her sweater to caress the heated flesh directly. When he found no bra strap, he paused, then began a slow glide over her ribs to her chest. She was so excited that her breasts ached before he finally took them in his palms. His hands made kneading motions, then rubbed in circles just at the tips. She moaned with pleasure.

Dev felt as if a curtain of fire enclosed them in a private place that was shielded from all others. It was almost beyond belief to finally have Lainie in his arms responding to his slightest touch with low moans and gasps of encouragement.

He wanted to bury himself in the soft heat of her, to feel her eager welcome. He knew how it would be. To make love with Lainie would fulfill a dream...at last.

He lifted his head and glanced around the dim stable. He couldn't take her there on the floor. He wanted to make their bed comfortable for her. A horse blanket in the straw? No, they should go to the house. Only smooth sheets and soft covers would do. He didn't want any scratches on her smooth skin.

"Come," he said hoarsely.

He stood, bringing her to her feet, too. The movement dislodged the ice pack that had numbed the bruise. A twinge of pain fought its way to his passion-drugged brain.

He realized what he was doing.

And what was that? Going crazy over a woman. Forgetting everything while he held her. Thinking only of her, of having her, of making their lovemaking perfect for her. Making a fool of himself, in other words.

He set her away from him, and the chilled air struck his bare legs. With a disgusted grimace he found his jeans and pulled them on, then his discarded boots.

"Be careful," Lainie warned in a husky voice. "I'll fix you an ice bag at the house. I know I saw one in the kitchen drawer the other day-"

"Forget it," he snapped. He flicked off the lantern and indicated that she should precede him out the door.

Her confused expression, coupled with the glaze of desire in her eyes, almost proved his undoing. He fought like hell to keep from taking her into his arms again. And if he did? He closed his eyes wearily.

Having once made love to Lainie, would he be like his father, always yearning for her when she was gone?

Lainie looked with consternation at Dev. One moment she had been embroiled in the most passionate kiss she had ever known, and the next she had been set aside like an unwelcome guest. Seeing the lines of fatigue and pain on his face reminded her of his injury and the fact that he had worked from sunup to sundown that day, as he usually did. He was probably ready to drop. A wave of sympathy flooded her.

"You should be in bed," she scolded. "Come on." She led the way to the house.

In the kitchen she flipped on the light over the sink and rummaged through the drawer where she'd seen the ice bag. Dev disappeared upstairs. She followed him in a few minutes.

At his door she hesitated, then knocked as quietly as possible. Tess, she knew, could sleep through a tornado. If the girl hadn't awakened during the stallions' screaming, she wasn't going to leap up at a few taps on a door at the opposite end of the hall.

There was no answer from inside. Lainie turned the knob and entered. A lamp had been turned on next to the bed, but Dev was nowhere to be seen. She decided that the thing to do was leave the ice bag on his pillow where he'd be sure to see it.

Just as she reached the bed, he walked out of the adjoining dressing room. He had stripped and washed. His hair was wet at the temples, and he swiped carelessly at his torso with a towel. He stopped when he saw her.

Lainie felt like a cat burglar caught in the act. She was still leaning to place the ice bag on the bed, her body bent in an awkward position as she took in the sight of his body…his magnificent *naked* body.

Before she could excuse herself and beat a hasty retreat, he was at her side, his hands reaching for her, his face a mask of fury. With one swift movement, he laid her on the king-size mattress and followed her down, his body covering hers with an urgent hunger that thrust her straight back to the level of desire she'd experienced in the stable.

His lips devoured her with wet, hot kisses all over her face and neck while his hands searched under her sweater. He made contact with her skin, and she thought the flesh would burn and fall right off her bones.

She knew she should resist him. For years she had kept him at a distance and her own traitorous emotions under control, but at this moment she just couldn't. Her hands went instinctively to his chest. For the first time she touched his bare torso and ran her fingers through the curly whorls of honey-brown hair. She could think of no reason to refuse this magic gift.

"Damn you, Lainie, and damn the crazy feelings I get whenever you're close." He pulled away from her with obvious effort. "Get out of here while you still can."

"I don't want to go," she said shamelessly. Surely he wouldn't deny them now, not when they were so close to fulfillment. But he did.

"Out," he said.

She levered herself up and off the bed while he grabbed a robe from the closet. She rushed to the door, the searing flames of rejection burning in her heart.

At the door she paused. Without looking at him she said, "Don't forget the ice pack. It'll help the swelling."

"Lainie, I..." He stopped on a sharply inhaled breath. "You'd better get some rest."

She closed the door behind her and ran soundlessly along the corridor. In her room she pressed her shaky hands over her face, not willing to believe how wanton she had been. She had told him she didn't want to leave him, had practically begged him to make love to her.

Where, she asked herself, was the cool, calm Lainie when she had needed her most?

Chapter Five

Lainie stared at her face in the mirror. She didn't feel like going to church this morning—maybe crawling in a hole, yes, but church, no. She smiled ruefully at her reflection. The action only emphasized the lines around her eyes and mouth. She felt every one of her thirty-three years today. After last night, who wouldn't?

Dev had sounded so grim when he had told her to get out of his room, but when she had complied he had said her name, *"Lainie,"* so oddly. Had there been despair in his voice? What had he been about to add? *Lainie, I…*want you? need you? love you?

She blinked as her eyes misted over. Dev had never spoken of love to her. From the moment they had met there had existed a current of awareness between them, but that was all. No Garrick male had ever spoken to her with tenderness.

Don't get melodramatic, she scolded and splashed water over her face until all traces of her sleepless night were gone. She had some decisions to make. First, she would stay one more week, then leave. Even Dev would see the sense of that.

He had been right to push her away last night, but there might come a time when both of them were weak at the same moment. Then where would they be? She couldn't face the regret and anger she would see in his eyes. She wasn't sure she could face him now.

Second, she would get her life together again. She had been a widow for eighteen months. Her husband had been ill for almost that long before he died. She had grieved enough. She was a person who needed people, not a lot of them, but a special person to share her life and dreams.

Glancing at the clock she saw it was time to quit playing the coward and go down to breakfast. To bolster her courage she dressed in a pimento-red dress with navy spectator pumps, and matching purse, then flung a white, red and navy scarf around her shoulders. She tied a jaunty knot in each of its two front corners. There, she looked ready to take on the world.

Only Agnes and Tess were in the kitchen when she entered. They exchanged greetings.

"You want waffles?" Agnes asked. "There's fresh juice in the pitcher."

"Waffles sound heavenly," Lainie said, glancing at the one rapidly disappearing from Tess' plate. She poured a glass of juice and stood by the sink looking out the window. The sunlight on the trees and grass was blindingly cheerful. "Where's Dev?"

"He's working today," Agnes told her. "Zed's gone to fetch a couple of the hands, and they're going to run the mustang into the highlands and away from the ranch."

"Oh, wonderful," Lainie exclaimed. When the other two looked at her in surprise she added, "I was afraid, that is, I thought he was going to shoot it or something."

"Dev would never do anything like that," Agnes informed her. The housekeeper looked indignant.

"What happened?" Tess demanded. She was dressed in a floral skirt and yellow blouse. Her make-up was light. She looked fresh and pretty.

Lainie explained the events of the night. While Agnes and Tess discussed the wild horse and the possibilities of catching it, Lainie rehashed the more intimate happenings between her and Dev. It was only natural that they should finish what Charles had interrupted so long ago. They had been curious about their reactions to each other.

Okay, so there was awareness between them. It was passion, some candid part of her chimed in. Yes, passion. But that was as far as it went. They'd gotten the kiss out of the way and no longer had to wonder about it.

Because now they knew, she concluded glumly. Passion, yes, but so wild and sweet that it made her blood sing just to remember. Had it been the same for him?

Lainie was hardly aware of eating the waffle that Agnes set in front of her. She remembered little of the ride to church except that Tess was driving. The church service was a blur. It was only when the three women were leaving that she was jolted out of introspection.

A blond separated herself from the crowd in the church yard and spoke to them. "Hi, I'm Marilynn Sikes," she said to Lainie. "You must be the sister from back East."

Lainie began to feel that "back East" was just this side of Mongolia, the way the local people referred to it. "Yes. I'm Lainie Alder."

"I'm glad to meet you." She turned to Agnes. "Tell Dev I've decided to sell him Morning Glory at the price we discussed last night. Ask him to give me a call tonight, or he can come over." She grinned. "If he wouldn't mind grilling the meat again, I'll feed him."

On the trip home Lainie kept seeing Dev at the grill and Marilynn in the house, setting a table for two with candles and fine china. Soft music played in the background.

Marilynn was very pretty. She had streaky blond

hair that looked natural, and a megawatt smile. Her eyes were mostly green with a subtle mix of light brown. Lainie guessed her age to be about twenty-five.

"I don't remember meeting Marilynn before," she remarked as they crossed the bridge over the wash. "Is she new around here?"

"Her dad bought the Chisholm ranch about a year ago," Tess said. "She's divorced."

Agnes filled in a bit more. "When her mother died last fall, she came home and stayed."

"I guess she felt she had to take care of her father," Lainie remarked, trying to be gracious about a beautiful blond only five miles away whom Dev had visited until midnight.

"I 'spect she felt she had to be near Dev. She's been trying to get him ever since she came," Agnes said. The housekeeper had an offhand way of getting right to the point in her observations on life.

"Well, she seemed nice," Lainie concluded.

"She is," Tess said. "She's chairman of the Frontier and Founders' Day celebration coming up this summer. She's great at organizing things."

Lainie was thankful for the information. It certainly helped to put her feet back on the ground and get her over her qualms about Dev and the kiss in the stable.

When the three women returned to the ranch Tess dropped Agnes at her house, then parked the car in the garage. The ranch house was empty when they entered.

"You want to swim, Lainie?" Tess asked.

Lainie agreed. Exercise would burn out the cobwebs in her brain. Perhaps she'd take a nap later.

She changed to her suit, then made sandwiches and a plastic jug of lemonade. She carried these out to the pool. When Tess arrived they swam, then ate their lunch. After the meal they lay on mats in the shade of a sycamore. The buffalo grass made a lumpy bed, but neither minded. Just when Lainie was about to drift into a nap, the telephone rang. Tess went to answer it.

She returned in a few minutes with the news that she was going to visit her friend Hilary, who was at Marilynn's house. Marilynn was the girl's aunt. "Is that okay with you? Would you mind being here alone?"

Lainie smiled up at the anxious expression on Tess' face. "Go ahead. I'm just going to be lazy all afternoon."

Tess dashed off to dress. A few minutes later, Lainie heard the station wagon crank up, then the *burrr* of the tires on the bridge. She closed her eyes and let sleep wash over her.

"You're going to burn."

Lainie pulled her senses together and sat up. Dev stood a couple of feet from her. He was dressed in a cowboy's working clothes—jeans, chambray shirt, boots and Stetson—and looked as handsome as the devil.

Glancing past him she saw how far the sun had shifted. She'd slept for several hours. "Did you run the stallion off?"

He shook his head. "He must have a hiding place somewhere close. Every time we get near, he disappears into a box canyon. I know there's no way out, so he has to be hidden."

"Umm," Lainie murmured, glad for the wild stallion. He'd been so beautiful in the moonlight trumpeting his challenge.

"I've decided not to capture him...if we can get him to go into the back country and keep away from the mares."

A sardonic smile curved his mouth into pleasant lines. Lainie felt her insides shimmer in response.

"Does that make you happy?" Dev asked. His voice dropped to a husky register as if he really cared about her happiness.

It was a good thing she had met Marilynn. The fact that Dev was seeing another woman would serve to keep her feet firmly planted on terra firma. "Yes. It seems wrong to tame such beauty. I know that sounds silly—"

"No, it doesn't." He frowned at her. "I understand the sentiment. All ranchers aren't hard-boiled and heartless. At times we can appreciate the finer things in life."

She stood and draped a towel around her. "I didn't mean to imply that you were. I don't really think you're insensitive. I apologize for saying that the other day."

They stared at each other and the air trembled with unspoken questions. His gaze ran over her, leaving her heated and bothered by his masculine perusal. It was madness to stay here.

"About last night—" he began.

"About staying here—" she started.

"You first," he said, making an impatient gesture.

"I've decided to leave at the end of the week. Tess will be working all summer. That should keep her occupied. If you'll just remember to talk to her instead of laying down the law, I think she'll cooperate. She's bright. She understands more than you give her credit for."

Dev didn't say anything for so long that Lainie thought she would scream. The tension knotted in her stomach and spread to her fingers. She clenched the towel tighter around her.

"Running, Lainie?" he asked. "Are you afraid I won't be able to control my baser instincts when you're around, especially dressed as you are now?" He gave a mirthless laugh. "You're probably right."

"Dev," she protested.

"Run back to Virginia. You'll be safe among the bloodless men there." With this strange pronouncement, he left.

Lainie sank onto the mat. The conversation had

somehow gotten out of hand and off track. She had wanted to inform him calmly of her plans and encourage him to be tactful with Tess.

"What bloodless men?" she muttered, angry at her inability to understand him. How had they gotten off the subject of Tess and onto her deficiencies, as he obviously saw them? Had he accused her of being a coward?

Well, she admitted ruefully, she was, wasn't she? She did want to run back home and be secluded from problems. Visiting the ranch had always been too difficult for her. It stirred up too many emotions she didn't want to think about.

"I am leaving," she said aloud in the direction Dev had taken.

At that moment a trumpet of rage tore the air. She looked up on the ridge. The Appaloosa stood there, his head lifted in a challenge. Stay free, she advised. Don't learn to love a man.

Lainie closed her eyes in despair. She loved Dev. So what else was new?

Tess went off to work on Monday in fair spirits. Lainie chewed her bottom lip but decided against saying anything about the high-heeled sandals. The girl would learn soon enough.

"Maybe you'd better go to town and have lunch with her," Agnes remarked. "And take her another pair of shoes."

Lainie smiled over the edge of her coffee cup. "I

remember my first day at work. It was in a bookstore. I wore my best clothes and highest heels...then spent the day unpacking books in the back room and checking computer printouts.''

At noon she went to town as Agnes suggested and carried Tess a pair of comfortable low shoes.

"Lainie, you're an angel,'' Tess said with a giant sigh when Lainie entered the store at noon.

"Care for some lunch?'' Lainie invited. "My treat.''

"Great. I'm starved,'' Tess said. She changed shoes. "Ahh, my arches thank you. My toes thank you. I have to stay until Dora gets back, then I have an hour. I'm off Wednesdays and Sundays and earn the minimum wage.''

"The place looks better,'' Lainie commented.

"I spent the morning dusting and rearranging. Dora was really pleased. She said I had an eye for color.''

"I agree.''

They went to lunch when Dora returned. After the meal Lainie spent a pleasant couple of hours chatting with the owner about the store while Tess cleaned each shelf of merchandise. When she looked at her watch, most of the afternoon was gone. "I've got to get back. Dev may need the truck.''

After she left the store she made a mental note to talk to Dev about the car she wanted for Tess. The teenager really needed one. Dev and Agnes couldn't share the pickup all summer.

On Wednesday Tess slept late. She entered the kitchen just as Lainie was finishing her second cup of coffee. "I'm going to spend the day with Hilary. She's visiting Marilynn. I'll be back late this afternoon." She turned to Agnes. "I'll hoe the garden when I get home, so don't worry about it."

She was gone in a few minutes. Lainie thought the house seemed empty without Tess' bubbling energy. Whatever else the girl was, no one could say she was lazy. Lainie decided to point that out to Dev and filed it with the question about the car.

The thought must have conjured the man. The back door opened, and Dev came in from the mud room where he left his boots. He was thoughtful about tracking up the house, she noted. The chill of the morning air clung to him making Lainie think of the winter to come.

The house would stand snug against the northern winds. A wood fire would burn each night in the den. Her mother had always popped enormous bowls of popcorn for them.

Lainie realized how lonesome she was for the little rites of family life. She was thirty-three. There wasn't all that much time left for her to establish a family.

Dev poured a cup of coffee and sat in his usual chair at the table. He flicked her a glance. "You up to a ride today?"

She was so stunned at the invitation that her voice

failed her. She nodded instead, wondering what he planned.

"I thought I'd explore that box canyon this morning, see if I can locate the mustang's hiding place and seal it off. Then I'll use the plane to run him over the Sycamore Canyon ridge to the open range," he explained.

He heard himself asking Lainie to join him and wondered if he had lost his mind. Since Saturday night he had avoided her as much as possible, leaving the house at sunup and not returning until late, then eating a warmed-over supper alone in the kitchen when he did. Damn, but he was tired. He couldn't keep up this pace forever.

Lainie was right. It was better that she leave. He couldn't think straight when she was around. Things had nearly gotten out of hand when he had kissed her. He shouldn't have done that. Now he knew how she felt, all woman soft and warm against him, and he wanted to kiss her again. He wanted a hell of a lot more than—

"But won't other ranchers take potshots at him then?" she interrupted his thoughts. "I mean, if he bothers their horses, isn't it legal to…to destroy him?"

Dev nodded. He took a drink of coffee. Lainie watched his throat work. It almost seemed a dream that she had lain against his chest and kissed the strong column of his neck in passion.

"He's wily," Dev said. "He's got a chance on the

range. If he stays here, I'll have to catch him and see if he can be tamed. Otherwise…'' He shrugged his shoulders.

"I'll come with you," she said.

An hour later she was in a western saddle, mounted on a friendly gelding. Her horse wasn't as large as the gelding Dev rode, but it could keep pace well enough. Dev wasn't taking any chances by riding a stallion to be challenged or a mare to be lured away, she saw.

They rode across flat bottom land, then up a narrow trail along the ridge until they came out on top.

"Oh, this is glorious," she exclaimed.

The view stretched for miles, and she could see fold upon fold of land winding away in all directions. The moment of creation seemed but a second ago the air was so clear. She saw a hawk riding a thermal above the valley. "Look," she said, pointing.

But Dev was looking at her, and there was such hunger on his face that she dropped her arm and sat very still. Like a rabbit in the presence of a predator, she thought. He blinked once and turned back to the trail, a heavy frown between his eyes.

She wondered if he knew he had given his thoughts away. He was remembering Saturday night, too. Was that why he had invited her to join him? He wanted to finish what had been started and denied? No, Dev wouldn't cold-bloodedly plan a seduction just to ease his physical needs. He wasn't that kind of man. What kind was he?

Her horse stumbled on the rough path, and she pushed the troubling thoughts aside and concentrated on the present. She was beginning to tire when he signaled a stop.

"Here's the mouth of the canyon," he said when she pulled up beside him. "I thought you could ride the eastern edge and I'd take the western. We'll meet where the creek starts in that stand of cottonwoods and have lunch."

Lainie's stomach rumbled at the mention of the food stored in his saddlebags. Agnes had packed them a hearty lunch.

"Okay," she said.

"Yell if you see the Appaloosa. I saw signs of him just a moment ago. He was through here in the last few minutes."

She had seen the patch of wet ground, too. Her gelding tossed his head and pulled the reins when she started around her half of the canyon. She rode slowly and dutifully kept a sharp eye on the rocks and shrubs for a hiding place. An hour later she met up with Dev. "No luck," she called.

"Me either," he said. "We'll eat in the shade."

Lainie pushed a wayward strand of hair behind her ear and tilted her face to the sun. She loved its warmth beaming down on her like a blessing. The canyon, with its harsh landscape of sage and bare dirt relieved by the scraggly cottonwoods around the tiny beginnings of the creek, seemed an enchanted place.

Feet back on the ground, she cautioned. She glanced around as if memorizing the place. Dev was already halfway to the shade trees. Just when she started to nudge the gelding down the steep trail to the valley floor, a movement caught her eye.

There, not fifty feet away, was the mustang. He stood in a narrow, angled fold of the canyon wall. A tree and several shrubs hid him from view in the opening. Only the fact that she was slightly above the fold allowed her to see into it and catch a glimpse of his ears twitching as he listened to the humans' talk.

With a pounding heart she kicked the gelding, and he leaped down the trail with an indignant toss of his head. She tied him next to Dev's horse where he could drink from the stream or munch the new grass to his heart's content. She joined Dev in the shade.

Her fingers trembled slightly as she accepted her sandwich from him. He filled a tin mug with coffee and held it out to her. He frowned at the tremor as she reached for it. "I should have realized this was too long a trip for you. You probably haven't ridden in years."

"Yes, I have. I ride with friends who own a horse farm in the country nearly every month."

He snorted. "That's a lot."

Her face reddened at his derisive comment, but she managed a smile. They'd better leave soon, or the mustang might get tired of waiting and bolt out of hiding. She took a big bite of chicken sandwich and downed it with a drink of coffee. The coffee burned her tongue. She ate more slowly.

"Where are your cattle?" she asked. She swallowed the last of her sandwich and finished the coffee.

"Some are out on the open range. Some are in the area, probably down at the main branch of the creek. They pretty much wander where they please during the summer."

"I see." She brushed hair out of her eyes. Was that a movement through the trees above them? She stood and paced to the creek and back. "Are you about through?"

"Yes." He finished a second sandwich and poured more coffee into his cup. He held the Thermos bottle out to her.

"No, thanks." She looked at her watch. "Should we be leaving? It's getting late. One o'clock."

"You got an appointment?" he asked. His tone was sardonic.

"Of course not. I just thought you were in a hurry."

He rinsed out their cups in the stream and packed them in the saddlebags again. "What in tarnation is wrong with you?" he demanded. His expression darkened. "If you're afraid of a repeat of Saturday night, don't worry. I have everything under control."

"No, it isn't that. It's just…" What could she say?

"We'd better go." He untied the horses and gave her a boost into the saddle before leaping on to his mount. "If you're tired, you can follow the trail back to the house."

"No, I'm fine."

They rode off out of the box canyon and along the main rim, the path taking them up to the top. Again she viewed the panorama of the world. Looking back, she saw the stallion.

He whickered as if telling her goodbye, then turned and raced away. Lainie lifted a hand and waved, a glad smile lighting her face.

"How did he get up there without us seeing him?" Dev muttered behind her. "That horse has more tricks than a carnival gypsy."

Lainie laughed. "He was hiding in the box canyon."

"He what?"

She realized what she had said. She faced Dev. "He was standing at the end of the canyon in a fold of rock that's hidden by the trees. I assume the creek starts out there."

Dev cast her a glance of pure annoyance. "I should have your hide for that. Why didn't you tell me?"

"I didn't want him to be caught."

He studied her for a long minute, then shook his head. "Show me this hiding place. I promise I won't try and catch him. I'll take the plane and drive him upcountry."

After they examined the crack in the rock they started on the trail for home, going directly across the ranch valley rather than following the rim trail. They crossed a ravine. A short distance on the other side, Dev muttered an expletive and dismounted. The fence that divided his property from the next ranch was down. He studied the terrain.

"Several cattle went through here. I wondered why we didn't see any along the creek. Do you mind riding over that way?" He nodded toward a distant clump of trees.

"No."

Mounting, he led the way at a lope. When he slowed and held up a hand, Lainie pulled the gelding to a stop. She heard a noise on the far side of the trees. The hair stood up on her neck. Rustlers?

"Stay here," Dev ordered. "I'm going to take a look."

He climbed down and headed for the small grove. Lainie followed right behind him. She was surprised when she saw two horses ground-hitched among the trees. The bay with white stockings looked familiar. She recognized the interwoven GCR brand of the Garrick Canyon Ranch. In a moment she knew why.

Tess was standing in a little clearing, facing a young man dressed in worn denims and a blue cotton shirt. They were looking at each other, their faces so full of longing and despair that Lainie's heart ached with pity for them. The young man reached out and touched Tess' cheek in a gentle caress.

Lainie glanced at Dev. He was furious.

"Strange place to meet your girlfriend for lunch,"

he announced. He strode out of the shade. Lainie stayed glued to his side. She didn't know what would happen, but she was determined to prevent bloodshed if possible.

The young man put Tess behind him and faced Dev squarely. He was almost as tall as Dev but hadn't yet filled out into the heavier frame of a fully mature man. He was slender in the manner of cowboys, wiry and strong-muscled, but with no extra ounces. His bone structure was clearly visible in his thin face.

Lainie admired his courage. She would have been quaking in her boots if Dev ever looked at her the way he was looking at Tess' friend.

"I thought I made it clear you were to stay away from Tess when I fired you," Dev said in an ominously quiet tone.

Lainie laid her hand on his sleeve. He flicked the barest glance her way, then looked back at the cowboy.

Tess spoke up. "Leave him alone. He didn't ask me to come here. I...he told me to stay away. I wanted to see him, to talk to him." She stopped, realizing that they hadn't exactly been discussing the weather or anything else when Dev stalked out of the woods.

"Go home, Tess," the young man said, pushing her gently aside.

"Carson—"

"You heard the man," Dev broke in.

"I suggest we all go home. We can discuss this another time," Lainie said firmly.

"You and Tess go. I'll catch up." Dev turned his head to give Tess a harsh glance. "I'll talk to you later."

When Carson didn't respond to her appealing glance, Tess walked from the site, her head high. In a moment the sound of her galloping horse echoed in the glen.

Lainie ignored Dev's order to leave. "Don't fight. You'll only make matters worse."

"I'm not going to fight him," Carson said.

Lainie studied them for a minute. She decided enough time had elapsed. Tempers had cooled slightly. "I'll wait with the horses." She walked back through the woods.

There was no sound of blows falling when she stopped near the grazing horses. Once she thought she heard the deep rumble of Dev's voice but wasn't sure. It was little more than five minutes, although it seemed an hour, before Dev joined her.

They swung into their saddles and started on the homeward path. Dev looked like a statue depicting silent fury.

"Don't be harsh with her," Lainie said. "She's already hurting."

Dev gave her a look that could have turned her to stone. "What is it about Debra and her daughters that drives men to obsession over them?" he demanded in a gritty voice.

''No one's ever been obsessed with me,'' she protested. Charles had adored Debra, Carson seemed to care greatly for Tess, but no man had ever offered his soul for her.

''Haven't they?'' There was no mistaking the sarcasm. ''Haven't they?'' he repeated in a softer tone that she couldn't decipher as his searing anger gave way to a less readable emotion but one that was just as fierce.

Chapter Six

Dev continued staring at her for another moment, then he spurred his horse and rode ahead, taking the lead the rest of the way home.

"Wait," she called. The implications of that terse question seemed vast. They needed to discuss the situation between them.

"Come on," he said over his shoulder. "We haven't time to discuss our problems. There's still Tess to deal with."

He was right. Lainie forced aside her own feelings and concentrated on Tess. Her sister had had as much emotional buffeting as she needed in one day. From the grim set of Dev's mouth when they reached the stable and dismounted, he planned to read her the riot act. But not if she could help it.

He opened a gate to one of the paddocks and

turned his horse in. Lainie followed him. Silently he removed the saddles while she slipped the bridles off. They carried the tack into the stable. When he started toward the door Lainie blocked his way.

"You're not going to talk to her in your present mood," she said. "You're too angry."

"Damn right I'm angry. She lied about where she was going. She knew the McCumber place was off limits."

"This isn't the army and you're not the general," Lainie told him. She stood her ground although she was trembling inside. "If you continue in this vein, you're going to make an enemy of Tess. You're her brother, not her warden. A few minutes ago, you spoke of dreams and feelings. Think of hers."

A flush crept under the tanned skin of his throat. "What I said...that was a long time ago."

"A time when you were close to Tess' age. Remember what it was like?" She delved into her own past and brought up the feelings. It wasn't hard. They were very akin to those she had now. "Remember the longing, Dev? Remember how you ached to see the other person? Do you remember—"

He clasped her upper arms and pulled her close. "Yes, I remember," he said. He spoke with deliberation, his voice soft and dangerous. "I remember nights of torture, knowing you were just across the hall. It might as well have been a mile. You retreated fast enough when my father appeared. You knew which side your bread was buttered on, didn't you, Lainie?''

He moved her aside as easily as a lump of clay. For a second she froze, almost as if she were paralyzed. Then she went after him.

She grabbed his arm, and he stopped and turned to her. The fury in his eyes should have dropped her on the spot, but her own anger was as great.

''Are you implying that I used Charles' guilt about me and his desire to protect his only son from my wiles to wheedle money out of him for school?'' She shook his arm. ''Are you?''

''Dammit, Lainie, I…no, I never meant that.'' He stepped closer to her. She released his arm and stepped back.

''What did you mean?''

''Nothing.'' He ran a hand over his face.

Lainie saw the lines of fatigue across his forehead and beside his mouth. Sympathy stirred. She brushed it aside. ''Why did you say it?''

''I wanted to hurt you.''

The stark truth of his statement hung between them.

''Why?'' she whispered. Never in a hundred years would she have described Dev as spiteful. What had she ever done to him to cause him to hate her so?

''Because you make me remember things I don't want to remember. Because you accuse me of harming Tess when I only mean to help her. I do have an inkling of what she's feeling. I want to protect her from that. She's young. She'll get over it or learn to live with the hurt.'' He paused to study Lainie's up-turned face. ''Just the way we all have to learn to survive in this world.'' He walked on toward the door.

Lainie fell into step with him. ''What are you go-ing to say to her?''

''Nothing.'' He sighed. ''I'll let you handle her. I said I would, and I meant it. You'll have to stay, at least for the summer,'' he added.

She had already realized that fact. She couldn't go off and leave Tess without a champion. The teenager was too volatile. Unlike Lainie, Tess acted on her feelings. There was no telling what she might do—run away, elope with a cowboy or the boy she had gone to the dance with—there were several possibil-ities.

''Will you?'' he asked.

The question surprised her. She summoned a wry smile. ''I thought it was decided already. The master has spoken.''

Dev shook his head. ''You're a puzzle, Lainie. One minute you're mad as an enraged bull, the next you're smiling as if nothing were wrong.'' He shook his head again.

''It's all part of the female mystique, Dev,'' she advised. ''Don't try to understand it.''

He studied her through narrowed eyes. ''Don't be cynical. One of us in that mood is enough.'' He reached for the doorknob, the gesture dismissive. ''I have work to do. There's a mare I want to buy for the stallion.''

''From Marilynn Sikes? I forgot about the mare. She mentioned it at church on Sunday.''

''Agnes told me Marilynn had changed her mind about selling.'' He looked pleased. ''That mare and the stallion I've been training will be the start of a string of show horses. The Garrick Ranch American-bred will be a name to be reckoned with.'' He went in, leaving her behind.

How simple life would be, Lainie, mused, if we could just buy a mate and have done with it.

Wrapping her arms around herself, she drifted to the pool and the solitude there. Although the day was hot, she felt cold inside, cold and wretched and lonely.

Had Dev once loved her? Was that what he had meant? Had she killed his love with her subsequent actions? She had become remote with him. She had spent less and less time at the ranch during the school vacations and between semesters during her college days. Knowing that Charles had threatened to send Dev away had forced her to pretend a coolness she didn't feel.

Had he really been hurt?

Lainie knocked on Tess' door. No sound came from within. She hadn't really expected an invitation to enter. She opened the door and went in.

Tess sat on a cedar chest and stared out the window. She didn't glance around when Lainie came in.

"I think we'd better talk," Lainie said. "Batting your head against a brick wall only hurts you."

Tess looked around then. Her face was red and puffy. She gazed back out the window. "Is life always like this?" she asked. Her voice was hoarse with tears.

Lainie chose her words carefully. "First love is, I think."

"When you met Con, and you two fell in love, did it...did it seem...sad and hurting?"

Lainie recognized the despair in Tess' voice. She thought back to her last year in college when Conrad Alder had given a series of lectures regarding entrepreneurship. She had been determined to start her own business and be independent from everyone. She had asked a thousand questions. He had talked to her at length after the classes.

Their relationship had started from a firm basis of friendship and deepened from there. It had never been sad or hurting or wildly sweet...

"No," she said in answer to Tess, "but sometimes it can be that way."

"What would you do if it were like that for you?"

"I guess it would depend on the problem. What do you see as the main obstacle to you and Carson?"

Tess sighed. "My age."

Lainie was surprised at Tess' insight. "Then you know it's something that time will take care of."

"Please, no lectures about my whole life being before me. I know all that. Dev has pointed it out more than once."

"Then give him credit for being right. And also for loving you very much."

Tess swiveled around at Lainie's harsher tone.

"He does love you, Tess. That means he cares about you and what happens to you. To love someone makes you responsible for that person, whether you want to be or not, just the way you tried to protect Carson from Dev's anger."

Pain flickered over Tess' face. "Carson said he didn't want me to bother him anymore. He said he had enough problems without an oversexed teenager on his hands. I've done everything he told me to. I've dated other boys. I've gone to all the school dances and everything." Her shoulders slumped. "It's no use. I want to be with him."

Lainie dropped down on the other end of the chest. Every young person, male and female, went through the throes of first love, she thought. There was no help for it, nor any cure but time.

Tess continued, "How long does it take to get over wanting someone who doesn't want you?"

"The way things looked when Dev and I came up, he must not have found you too repulsive," Lainie reminded her.

A faint blush colored Tess' cheeks. "I suppose he wants me like that, but he says he can't afford to get mixed up with me, that I'm too young to know what

I want, and he doesn't intend to make an enemy of Dev.''

"Carson's right. Dev would skin him alive if he took advantage of your feelings. If Carson won't declare himself, there's nothing you can do.''

"He would if things were different," Tess cried. "Next year I'll be eighteen and out of school. That's not so long to wait, but he says I'll have college after that.''

"That's true. Dev would never consent to your marrying without having tried your wings first. You need to get away from home, see something of the world and meet other people before you make up your mind.''

Tess made a grimace of disgust. "I should have known you'd be on their side.''

"No," Lainie corrected. "I'm not on anybody's side, but I see more clearly than you do right now. If you and Carson truly love each other, that love will still be there when you're ready for it. In the meantime, you owe Dev loyalty. Don't cast him as the villain in your life because you need someone to blame for your unhappiness. It's not fair to use him like that.''

Leaving Tess to think that over, Lainie went to her room. She lay on the bed feeling storm-tossed and weary. Had she helped matters or made them worse? Only time would tell.

Glancing at the clock she realized that it was nearly six. She rushed to the bathroom and took a quick shower. Coming out in her robe with her hair in a towel she met Dev in the hallway.

"Did you talk to Tess?" he asked, keeping his voice low.

"Yes."

He waited.

"I don't know how she feels. You'll have to be patient." She fiddled with the belt of her robe. "Don't come down on her like an angry father. She's your sister, an equal in status if not in age. Be patient and don't make her hate you."

"Is that the way you see me, as a person who's heavy-handed and runs over others' feelings?"

"I see you as a wonderful person who loves his family very much. You're not about to stand aside and let Tess make a mess of her life. But she's almost grown, Dev. She has to make some mistakes on her own."

"Not this one."

"I think Carson has taken care of that. He's a more sensible young man than we gave him credit for. I take it he was the one she went to the motel with?"

Dev nodded.

"I suspect she followed him there. From what she's told me about him, he wouldn't have invited her."

"He wasn't exactly loading her on her horse and sending her home when we found them today."

Lainie smiled. "Well, he's human. Even you give in to nature on occasion, Dev." Tension hummed in the air as she boldly reminded him of their indiscretion.

He touched her cheek. "Only when you're around, Lainie."

Lainie wielded the hoe with vigor. She was restless.

"Those are radishes you're tearing through," Agnes remarked.

Lainie looked closely at the weeds she'd been attacking. "Oh, I'm sorry, Agnes. I'll see if I can salvage any for lunch."

She knelt on one knee and searched the soil for the bulbs. She retrieved several.

"Things sure are quiet around here these days," Agnes said in her usual dry way of getting right to the point.

"Yes, the white flags are out."

"Wonder how long it's going to last? I can't imagine Dev or Tess holding everything in for long."

"Are you warning me to expect another explosion soon?" Lainie asked. A wry smile accompanied the question. She sometimes felt that they were living on the edge of a volcano known to erupt every fifty years and this was the fifty-first year since the last eruption.

"Well, just be prepared."

The two women exchanged sympathetic glances.

"I'm going in to put these greens on to boil. Don't stay out in the sun too long."

Lainie said she'd be careful. She pulled the brim of her borrowed straw hat lower on her forehead and went on weeding. There was something satisfying about physical work, she reflected, especially if the results were seen right away. She looked back at the neat row of vegetables behind her. They had had several light rains during the month and the weeds had taken hold.

She sighed. June was in its last week. She'd been in Arizona for four weeks. The store in Virginia Beach was doing fine. She had decided to let her manager make the decisions on new stock and see how it went. Perhaps she would invite her to become a partner.

A shadow fell across the row.

"You'll get sunstroke," Dev advised.

She looked up and, using his gesture, pushed her hat back a little so she could see him better. "It's not that hot."

"It's nearly midday. You should rest in the shade."

"That's all I've been doing for a month, resting." She grimaced with distaste. "Besides, haven't you heard—hard work makes for peaceful dreams?"

She needed whatever she could find to make her sleep so she wouldn't lie awake thinking of the way his hands had felt, rough and gentle as he caressed her.

"You need something to do," he concluded. "You're used to being busy."

"Right. I guess I'm just not a vacation person. When I go on a trip, it's to buy stock for the store. I like that much better than lying around or looking at museums."

"Hmm," he said. "I might think of something. By the way, I've found a car for Tess in Clarkdale. You want to drive in and take a look this evening?"

"Yes," she exclaimed. "What kind is it?"

"You'll see." He grinned, obviously pleased with his find.

She frowned after him when he strolled off. What was he planning? He'd been true to his word about letting her handle Tess, so things had smoothed over somewhat. All's quiet on the western front, she thought. But for how long? She finished the gardening and returned the hoe to the shed, then went in to help Agnes with lunch.

Since it was Friday Tess would be working late in the store. Agnes had plans to go to a movie with another widowed friend.

"Why don't we have dinner after we look at the car?" Dev asked. "I haven't been to my favorite restaurant in weeks."

"That would be fine," Lainie agreed. She realized then she had never been to a restaurant with Dev in all the years she'd known him. It seemed strange to even think of it.

Later, when she looked through her closet after her shower, she couldn't decide what to wear. This isn't a date, she reminded herself when she pulled out a black silk dinner dress. She put it back and took down a pink cotton dress that was fresh and sweet-looking. After considering a minute or two, she put it back. She'd think about it while she dried her hair.

When she went down the steps thirty minutes later, the black silk swished sensuously about her legs. She was glad she had put it on. Dev was wearing a dark summer suit of impeccable cut. He looked like a corporate CEO rather than a hardworking rancher.

In fact he was, she realized upon further thought. Charles had invested in mining and oil wells plus a couple of motel chains, as well as in land. Her earnings from the Garrick holdings were substantial. Dev handled the many decisions regarding those enterprises as the trustee for the estate.

"Ready?" he asked when she stood on a level with him. "Do you have a coat? You'll need one later tonight."

"I have a wool cape. I'll get it."

"No, wait. There's something here that Debra said you were to have. I forgot to send it to you."

He ran lightly up the steps and along the corridor to his room. In a minute he returned with a mink wrap. He laid it around her shoulders.

"Oh, it's beautiful." Lainie rubbed her cheek against the fur. "Did you know mink has six hundred thousand hairs per square inch?" she asked with a teasing smile. She was going to relax and enjoy the evening. If she wanted to fantasize that she was on a date with Dev, it was nobody's business but hers.

"How interesting," he murmured. "What other facts does your busy little brain hold?"

"Lots."

He took her arm and led her to the truck. "Your chariot awaits," he said with a mocking grin.

She couldn't make the large step in her fitted skirt. Placing his hands around her waist, he easily lifted her in. "You don't weigh as much as thistledown. I thought Agnes said she was going to fatten you up," he said when he climbed in and started off.

"She is. I've gained five pounds. If I don't watch it, I'll look like a dumpling."

"You look damned good and you know it."

Nothing like a compliment that sounded like an insult, she thought waspishly. She cast a glance at Dev. He met her look with one of his own. "Thank you," she finally said.

He laughed. "That cost you."

"Sometimes you could act as if you didn't know what I was thinking," she said in exasperation.

"Let's enjoy the evening."

She considered arguing with him about who was spoiling the mood but decided against it. After all, she had decided to have a good time, hadn't she?

Dev kept her in suspense about the car until they were on the used car lot. He lifted her out of the truck just as the salesman rushed over and shook hands as though Dev were a long lost friend, then he led the way around the building.

"Here she is," he announced. "Prettiest little filly we've had on the lot in a coon's age."

The car was a red Mustang, one of the earlier ones, but in excellent condition. It had recently been upholstered and painted.

"A Mustang," she exclaimed. She looked at Dev.

"You seem to be partial to the beasts," he drawled. A smile played at the corners of his mouth, and her heart increased its tempo.

"It's perfect." She walked around it, looking for flaws, then opened the door and sat in the driver's seat. The keys were in the ignition. She couldn't resist. "How about a test drive?"

The engine fired as soon as she turned it on. Dev climbed into the passenger seat, and Lainie took off. Out on the highway the car performed smoothly and handled well. She put it through its paces thoroughly.

"Where did you learn to drive like that?" Dev asked when they pulled into the car lot again.

She grinned. "I dated a guy who was into drag racing one summer. He taught me. I'll take it," she said to the salesman who dashed over to open her door almost before she stopped.

They signed the papers, and she wrote a check for the entire amount. "I'll ride into town with Tess on Monday," Lainie decided. "That way I can drive the Mustang home and have it there for her birthday dinner that night. I can't wait to see her face!"

Dev smiled in his slow, lazy way that could drive an unsuspecting heart right over the edge. Lainie schooled hers to caution. She was mature enough to handle desire, and she knew he felt that for her, but there were other things she wanted from a lover, she realized. More and more she was feeling the emptiness in her life. So many pieces were missing....

"What?" she asked.

"I asked, are you ready to go to dinner? Our reservations are for eight. I thought we'd have a drink before we ate."

"Yes, that's fine."

He lifted her into the truck, his hands strong and steady on her waist. Hands a woman could trust, she thought. When he lifted her down at the restaurant a few minutes later, she had to fight an impulse to put her arms around his neck and pull him closer.

She wondered if he read the thought in her eyes for his darkened as if in response. The two of them were volatile around each other. They struck sparks. How much longer before neither could resist the flames?

His hand touched the small of her back as they threaded their way to a cocktail table in the bar. Dev hadn't had to mention his name at the desk. The hostess had recognized him at once. Lainie realized she was jealous of the other women he had brought here.

She sighed as she sat down and let the mink glide sensuously off her shoulders onto the back of the chair. This would not do at all, she cautioned herself. She had no rights where Dev was concerned. She never had.

"Wine?" he asked.

She nodded, then listened to the quiet sound of his order over the babble of other couples around them. She was very vulnerable to him tonight. She loved the rich cadence of his baritone, the scent of his after-shave, the stubborn cowlick that caused his hair to wing outward before dipping into a sexy wave on his forehead.

When the waitress brought their drinks, she sipped the wine slowly, savoring the smoky flavor of *fume blanc*. For himself, Dev had chosen Scotch.

"I have something for you," he said, placing his glass on the table. He reached into an inner pocket of his suit and extracted a legal-looking paper. He held it out to her.

Lainie felt more than a little trepidation in taking it. When she read the title and skimmed the paragraphs, she realized it was a bill of sale. Dev had bought the gift shop...for her, as trustee of his father's estate.

"Why?" she asked, folding the document and laying it on the table between them.

"You're restless. You need a challenge to occupy your mind."

"I'll only be here another month, perhaps two," she added as a frown formed between his eyes.

"Tess needs you." He was silent. Then, "It's a gift, Lainie. I know it isn't much, but I want you to have it. *I* need to give you something to make up for all the unhappy years you spent at the ranch."

He was so humble that she couldn't bear it. "I'll think about it," she compromised, knowing she should refuse and take the first plane home. She was getting in too deep. The only way out was through heartbreak.

"If it wasn't my father that kept you away, was it me?"

She stared at him.

"Did I frighten you with my...desire? You must have known that I wanted to drag you off to the stable and finish what we had started there every time you visited." He looked directly at her. "Didn't you?"

She nodded. With trembling fingers she reached up to push a strand of hair off her face. She should have her hair cut, she thought inanely. She was too old to have it dangling around her shoulders all the time.

Dev leaned forward and tucked the errant curl behind her ear. He took her hand in his. His skin was so warm; hers was so cold.

"Did it frighten you?" he asked softly.

"No," she whispered. "I was never afraid of you." It was her own turbulent feelings that had scared her.

"Then you'll stay, at least for a while?"

"All right."

He picked up the bill of sale and stuck it back in his pocket. "For safekeeping," he told her. His grin was wry.

The hostess came for them and led them to a table. Lainie soon found herself laughing as Dev recounted his problems with cows and cowboys. "And the paperwork," he groaned. "One year the government asked us to keep track of all the forms we had to fill out in order to reduce the number. At the end of the year, they decided to cut the tracking form and keep all the rest."

Lainie grinned at his exaggerated sigh. She knew about filing forms and keeping records.

"Say, you wouldn't be willing to take over some of it, would you?" he asked hopefully.

She shook her head. "I have a shop to run, remember?"

"Yeah." His glance was warm.

Why shouldn't it be? He'd gotten his way, she mused, not sure whether to be chagrined or not. Keep your feet on the ground, she advised ruthlessly.

When he asked her to dance she repeated the admonition several times. It did no good. Before the second number ended she was cradled against his firm body, lost in dreams.

They drove home without talking. The touch of his hands still warmed her waist from his lifting her into the truck. He was strong, she thought dreamily. A man you could depend on.

At the house they had a nightcap before retiring. Tess came home and joined them in the den. She told them about her day. "I sold six of the cutest figurines. They're shepherdesses."

Lainie decided she'd better learn more about the clientele in the area before she attempted any large orders. She was obviously off in her judgment of their buying habits.

When Tess yawned and said good night, Lainie rose, too. "Thanks for dinner. It was wonderful," she said to Dev. "And thanks for the store. I think."

"What store?" Tess demanded, looking from one to the other.

Dev grinned. "Meet your new boss," he said.

"What?"

"Dev bought the gift shop in my name," Lainie explained.

Tess' eyes lit up. She hugged Lainie. "That must mean you're staying. Great! Oh, Lainie, I have some super ideas. What do you think about…"

Lainie glanced once over her shoulder as she left the room with Tess. Dev stood in the lamplight, his hair reflecting the light with a golden glow. In his eyes was the longing of a man for something beyond his grasp. Lainie couldn't help but wonder if he really wanted her as much as his expression indicated.

And if he did, why did it make him angry?

Chapter Seven

"I can't believe you own the shop," Tess said. She pulled into a parking space and turned off the engine. Lainie was following the plan of riding into town with Tess and returning with Dev. She intended to drive the birthday Mustang home.

"Me, either," Lainie said with a droll smile. She pointed to the Monday shoppers already checking the sales. "Look at the people," she remarked. "At my store…at my *other* store, the vacationers don't mosey out until around noon."

She pretended to look around, but in reality she was studying Tess. The girl was composed and quiet. None of the bubbling emotion normally so close to the surface appeared on her face. She was growing up and learning to hide her feelings, Lainie concluded. She felt sad all at once. Why did the young have to be hurt?

"Lainie, are you going to live here? At the ranch, I mean?" Tess looked at her with a silent plea.

"I don't know," Lainie answered honestly.

They got out of the car and walked toward the store when Dora appeared to open the shop.

Lainie murmured in an aside to Tess, "Rule number one: Don't be late or your customers will think you're not reliable." She paused, then added, "I have the town house in Virginia beach—"

"Sell it," Tess said, disposing of Lainie's home in two words.

"Maybe I'll make you manager here while I take care of things back East," Lainie suggested.

Tess shook her head. "I'll be leaving for college when I get out of school."

"You've decided to go?"

"Oh, yes. I'm going."

Tess looked so grim, as if going to college was a prison sentence, that Lainie had to hold back tears. Had her own eyes been so bleak when she went off to boarding school?

"I'll study psychology," Tess continued. A sardonic grin turned up the corners of her mouth. "Then maybe I'll learn to understand hardheaded ranchers."

"Don't waste your time," Lainie advised.

Their eyes met. A friendship was established and a bond forged that each recognized would last a lifetime.

"I'm glad you're home, Lainie," Tess said.

"Me, too."

The morning was spent discussing the store and its customers. Dora was a fountain of information. "Mrs. Crowder, the principal's wife, hates the mayor's wife, so don't let her buy something the other has already bought. Oh, and Clancy Smith is buying his wife a set of month plates, one each anniversary. He's up to November."

"I can't keep all this straight," Lainie protested with a laugh. "My head is in a whirl."

Tess had no such problem. She knew all the women. "I'll write it all down."

At noon Dev stuck his head in the door. "Ready to go? I thought I'd take you two out to lunch before we go home."

"I have to work," Tess said. She didn't look at him.

"Get along," Dora said. "I'll go after you get back."

But Tess refused, so Lainie and Dev ate lunch at a local café before picking up the Mustang. The atmosphere was strained.

"Tess hasn't forgiven me," he said near the end of the meal. "At least you two seem to be getting along." He rubbed his brow, and Lainie noted that he seemed tired. He was once again rising at dawn and working until dark.

"Yes, I think we're developing a closeness we've never had."

He looked at her intently. "I was right about your coming home. She needed a woman to confide in."

"She needed someone to listen," Lainie corrected. She spoke gently. "I think you two were too close. You needed an outsider to see that your love for each other was part of the problem."

His expression hardened. "Why do you always see yourself as an outsider?" he suddenly demanded. "Like it or not, you're family. Did you resent Debra's marriage to my father that much?"

"No. I was very glad for them."

"I wish I could figure you out," he finally muttered after staring at her as if she were a laboratory specimen.

"That goes double for me," she snapped. "You're the most changeable person I've ever met. I'm glad I don't have to live with you. No wonder Tess is confused about life and men."

The way she said *men* left no doubt in her listener's mind regarding her feelings toward the male sex.

"You've never stayed around long enough to know me, as a man or anything else," he replied, settling back in his chair with a sardonic twist to his smile.

"It doesn't take a lot of time to recognize a jackass when I meet one." She gave him a lofty glance, then pressed her lips together, not sure whether to laugh or run at the look that came over his face.

"Is that your opinion of me?" Dev asked with

deceptive softness. He signaled for the check and turned back to her with a motion that indicated temper rigidly controlled.

"No." Lainie smiled at his surprise. "I'm sorry, but you make me angry. We seem to bring out the worst in each other. Let's get the car and go home. Agnes said I could bake the cake for Tess' birthday dinner."

He paid the bill and drove her to the lot where Tess' car was parked. Waving her on he followed her out to the ranch. By the time the fifty-minute drive was over, she felt as if she should have two burning holes in the back of her head. Dev drove the pickup around the house and out of sight.

She wiped the road dust off the bright red Mustang and tied a big bow on the radio antenna. Leaving it right in front where Tess would see it upon arriving, she went in to bake the cake.

"Yellow butter cake with heavenly hash icing," she announced grandly to Agnes a couple of hours later. The icing was a favorite of Tess'—whipped cream with instant vanilla pudding, mandarin oranges, pineapple bits and maraschino cherries stirred in, the confection spread between three layers of cake.

"You have a good memory," Agnes complimented. "Of course you were always like that. You knew what made other people happy and tried to provide it for them. 'Bout time you took a little for yourself, isn't it?"

"You make me sound like some kind of saint. Should I apply for my halo now?" Lainie quipped to hide the rise of emotion. Agnes saw too much.

"No, go read or something while I get the rest of supper on. I can't stand another person in the kitchen."

"Yes, ma'am," Lainie said, beating a quick retreat. She decided to go for a swim and relax.

The store needed a lot of work. Dora had been quite gleeful when she admitted as much to Tess and Lainie. The older woman had confided that this would be her last week.

"You don't need me around to tell you what to do. I can see you're itching to get at it," she had observed.

She'd been right, Lainie admitted a few minutes later, lying in the shallow end of the pool, up to her neck in the soothing hot springs. Like Agnes, who preferred to have the kitchen to herself, Lainie had her own ideas for the store. She would have hesitated to execute them with Dora around. The changes might seem to disparage the other woman's way of doing things.

An eagerness to get moving on her plans filled her with restless energy. Dev had been right. She needed something to occupy her mind. The shop was a challenge that excited her.

"May I join you?"

She opened her eyes and looked up. Dev was standing on the ledge they used as a diving platform.

When she nodded he raised his arms and leaped into the deep end. Closing her eyes again, Lainie listened to the splashes of his swimming strokes. When the noise stopped she opened her eyes to see where he was.

He was swimming toward her with an underwater stroke that made no sound. When he could touch bottom, he walked to her end of the pool and settled himself beside her. Resting his head on his arms, he stared up at the shifting leaves that formed a canopy over their heads. Finally, he yawned and closed his eyes.

Lainie stole several peeks while he relaxed.

"Have my ears grown to full size?" he asked.

"What?"

"I thought maybe my ears had sprouted since I last looked. Jackasses have long ears, don't they?"

"Yes, and they bray a lot."

Grinning, she started to get out but a large hand clamped around her ankle. The next thing she knew the world was upside down, then it disappeared altogether as she went under water.

"Dev," she yelled when she surfaced. He knew she hated to be ducked. Now her hair was all wet. She'd have to spend an hour drying it and curling it away from her face to keep it out of her eyes during dinner. "I'm going to kill you for that."

"Catch me," he taunted.

She flailed the water for all she was worth, but he kept maddeningly just beyond her reach. She gave up and pulled herself up on the edge. He came over and held onto the rock ledge at each side of her legs, his grin daring her to do anything about it.

"Feel better now?" he asked.

Her glance was cool. "Better?"

"You were restless before."

"I was nearly asleep when you disturbed me."

"Restless," he repeated. He was stubborn.

She sighed, then smiled at him. "Yes, I feel better."

Their glances met and held. He stared steadily up into her face, the teasing expression in his eyes changing slowly to a deeper emotion, one that she recognized.

"I think I'll dry in the sun before I go in," she said. When she tried to move, her knee bumped his chest. Suddenly he was pressing against her, his hands sliding up her thighs to her waist. He lifted her into the water.

His hands still held her, but their bodies didn't touch. "I shouldn't do this," he murmured. "But I'm going to."

She couldn't stand the waiting. Lifting her arms she dripped water over his shoulders as she enclosed them. The space between them disappeared, and flesh burned against flesh. She wouldn't have been surprised to see steam rise from the water.

His lips covered hers in a hard, impatient kiss. He demanded further intimacy with the probing of his tongue. She parted her lips and gave him entrance, meeting his every stroke with one of her own. The sweet moist torture of his tongue on hers drove all thoughts from her mind except one. She wanted his entire touch. She wanted complete fulfillment in his arms.

When his hands moved along her back and slipped under the straps of her suit, she moved slightly. The straps fell off her shoulders. The material of the suit drifted down into the water. Then she felt the wonder of his heated flesh against her breasts.

He trailed kisses from her mouth to her ear and down her neck, then farther. With the gentlest of touches he kissed each raised nipple before taking it into his mouth and nibbling sensuously.

"Ah, Lainie," he breathed. "I never thought to taste such sweetness."

He sucked at the tender tips. He rubbed his face over her breasts as if he wanted to experience the wonder of touching her in all the ways there were.

She offered no resistance when he carried her to the shallows and sat on a boulder with her planted firmly across his lap. With hands on her hips, he pulled her against him. She gasped with the force of the passion he stirred in her when she felt the rigid desire in him. She moved instinctively against him, the warm water lapping with little suckling noises between them.

He devoured her with his eyes before reaching up to cup her breasts in his hands. Bending, he kissed each nipple again, then pulled her tight to him while his mouth sought hers.

They kissed until they were breathless and on fire with longing. Yet it was tender, too. There was such concern in his touch. Dev would never be harsh with a woman, she realized. However provoked, he would never lose control.

With the softest of touches to express her love, she caressed him, running her fingers through his thick, sun-streaked hair, sliding her palms over his shoulders, exploring the muscles of his strong back. Dev, oh, love, love…

Even as she thought the words she knew she could never say them. Nor could she take the gift of his body. It would never be enough for her, and she couldn't beg for more. If he didn't love her, he didn't. That was the way things were.

With lingering touches she slowly let the built-up passion subside until he raised his head and stared into her eyes.

"Don't say no," he murmured hoarsely.

"I have to." She touched his face, memorizing each plane and angle, each line that denoted care and responsibility. Love, love…

She withheld the words and controlled the passion until he saw she meant it. He sighed and a curtain came down over his face.

"You're right. What use to start something that has no good end?" He lifted her away from him and steadied her as she stepped from the pool. He turned onto his back and swam away from her. The evidence of his desire tempted her to call him back. Turning, she walked with her head down until she reached the house.

July was ushered in with fireworks on the Fourth followed by Frontier Days, a celebration of the pioneer spirit that had settled the West. The grand finale to the two-week-long festivities was a dance held on the street in the middle of town.

Lainie stood on the curb and watched the fun as couples square-danced.

"Ladies go left an' gents go right; swing that gal with all your might," the caller directed the dance in a sing-song voice. The dance ended, and the band struck up a Texas two-step before the street cleared.

"Come on, little lady, no use standing around looking lonesome."

A cowboy grabbed Lainie's wrist and led her into the street. He gave her a rakish grin and tipped his hat. "Anthony Archer at your service, ma'am."

"Lainie Alder," she responded with a curtsy.

"I knew we had something in common. Our last names both start with an A."

"That's significant, I'm sure," she said, laughing up at him.

He had hair as dark as hers, and gray eyes so light they looked as though they were made from crystal. He was obviously feeling good. "Look," he said, lifting the lock of hair off his forehead. He, too, had a widow's peak, although not as pronounced as hers. "Somewhere along the line, we must have a common ancestor."

She nodded. They joined the circle of dancers and began the two-step. She had learned it from her first roommate in college, who had been from San Antonio. When the cowboy saw that she knew the dance, he tried some fancy steps with her.

"Damn, a woman who can keep up," he said, pleased.

Lainie felt herself relax. At the periphery of the crowd she spotted Tess talking to Hilary and waved at the girls. A little farther along she saw Dev talking to Marilynn Sikes.

He had bought the mare from the woman and brought it home the previous week. Lainie had been disappointed. She had expected a beautiful horse but the mare was like the young stallion—a shiny brown with a darker mane and tail, nice but not spectacular. Personally, she thought the Appaloosa was the prettiest.

Dev laughed at something Marilynn was saying, and Lainie saw the woman lay her hand on his arm. Marilynn had detained him the same way, with the tips of her fingers laid gently on his arm, when Dev, Lainie and Agnes had arrived. Tess had driven in earlier and picked up her friend, Hilary.

Anthony whirled her around. "Hey, I'm your partner. You're supposed to look at me sorta like you're smitten and all that."

Lainie composed her face. "I'm sorry. I'll try to do better. How's this?" She gazed up at him, her eyes wide and adoring.

"Wow," he exclaimed, "you got it."

Pulling her to him he spun them around at the end of the music, then let her go. "That was lovely," she said, heading for her curbside viewing point.

"If you aren't spoken for," he began.

"She is," a deep voice said behind them.

Dev gave Anthony a cool perusal before glancing at Lainie. His possessive tone made her furious. She wasn't a mare he had to protect from a wayward stallion.

Forcing a light laugh as if she thought he was joking, she introduced the men. "This is Dev Garrick, my stepbrother. Dev, Anthony Archer. Anthony and I think we're long-lost cousins."

That startled Dev. "What makes you think that?" he drawled. His eyes narrowed as he studied first one, then the other.

"Besides the obvious—hair, widow's peak, similar names—we're kindred spirits. I recognized it right off." Anthony tipped his hat to her. "Save me a waltz for later, cuz." With a wink he swaggered off.

Lainie laughed when she saw him head toward Hilary and Tess. He was a flirt, but a harmless one. "Where's your friend?" she asked, glancing up at Dev.

"Who?"

She noted the tension in the set of his shoulders and wondered if he and Marilynn had quarreled.

"Marilynn."

"Oh, her," he said, dismissing the woman with a shrug. "I don't know."

Lainie smiled, a gladness sneaking into her heart that didn't belong there. She had no right to be jealous of the women in his life. Her eyes followed his. She saw that he was watching Anthony lead Hilary into a forming square while another young man grabbed Tess and pulled her into the same group. A startling thought jolted her. Had Dev been jealous of Anthony and her?

"Shall we dance?" she asked. Feeling bold, perhaps even brazen, she gave Dev a darting glance from beneath her lashes and was rewarded with the sudden expansion of his chest as he breathed deeply and let it out slowly. She found she wanted to taunt him for neglecting her in favor of the divorcée when they arrived.

"Let's have something to drink," he said. Placing his hand against her back he escorted her to a drink concession farther along the street. He ordered wine for her, a beer for himself.

Lainie sipped the wine from a paper cup, then laughed. She held the cup up. "The height of elegance." Again she let her eyes flirt with Dev.

"Come on."

Taking her free hand he guided them through the

crowd until they stood under a small tree in front of her shop.

"How's the store doing?" he asked. He hadn't been near the place since she had taken over two weeks ago.

"Checking on your investment?" she questioned. She felt her mood going sour and strove to regain it. "Stop by and find out sometime." She finished the wine and handed him the empty cup just as the cowboy swaggered her way.

"This is our dance," Anthony said, pulling her into his arms. With a grand flourish, he waltzed her into the street.

"For a cowboy, you dance wonderfully," she complimented him when he danced her into a promenade, then turned, and went into another promenade.

"My mom made me take dancing lessons." He made a woeful face.

"Archer," Lainie said. "Archer...as in Mayor Archer?"

"My father," he confessed. "Keep it mum."

She admired his jeans, plaid shirt and boots that had been shined but still showed the signs of wear. "You fill the part of a cowboy well."

"I'm home from the university for the summer and working at a ranch out near the Garrick spread. You know the McCumber place?"

"Oh, yes, I certainly do," she said.

Before he could question her tone the music ended, and another cowboy tapped him on the shoulder. The new partner said his name was Tom and he was pleased to meet her. "You the new owner of the store over there?" He nodded toward the gift shop where Dev stood looking like a thundercloud.

Lainie noted that he was drinking another beer, a different brand from the first one. She had never seen him drink more than one of anything in her life. When she smiled at him over Tom's shoulder, he glowered at her.

As the evening wore on the frown on Dev's face became more thunderous. Lainie had long ago decided to ignore him. Let him stand under the tree and scowl all he wanted. If he wanted to speak to her he could ask her to dance. Meanwhile, she danced with several partners and flirted lightly with Anthony in a jesting manner each time he ambled back to her between dances with other women, mostly Hilary and Tess.

"You seem to be enjoying yourself," she commented after one breathless reel.

"Umm-hmm. I think your stepbrother doesn't like me." With a laugh he waltzed her over to the tree and then, right on the other side of the trunk, kissed her in plain sight.

Lainie instinctively made a sound of protest. That apparently was all Dev needed. His hand clamped down on Anthony's shoulder and spun him around.

"I don't think the lady wants to be bothered by you anymore, cowboy. Beat it."

Anthony smiled devilishly. "Why don't you let

her speak for herself?'' he suggested, stepping away from Dev's grasp.

''She did,'' Dev snarled.

''Dev!'' Lainie said, keeping her voice low. She didn't want a scene.

''Keep out of this, Lainie,'' he ordered.

''I can take care of myself. I don't need you to *save* me.'' They glared at each other, forgetting the other participant.

''Ah, a two-step,'' Anthony said. ''My dance, I believe.''

Before he could sweep her into his arms, Dev swung at him. At the same moment Lainie stepped forward and Anthony politely moved back and took her arm. Dev's swing went wild, swiping nothing but air.

For a second he hung in an arc over her before settling back on his heels and dropping his fist. She stared at him, astounded at his action.

''Sorry,'' he muttered.

''You've been drinking,'' she said in disgust. ''We're going home right now. I'll tell Tess to bring Agnes.'' She smiled grimly at Anthony. ''Perhaps I'll see you another time.''

''You will,'' he promised.

With a silent Dev in tow she found Tess and told her they were leaving. Tess looked from one to the other and nodded without asking questions. ''I'll find Agnes. Don't worry about us.''

''Give me the keys,'' Lainie said when they

reached the station wagon. She held out her hand for them. With a slight grin that she couldn't begin to analyze, Dev dug into his jeans and handed over the keys.

They started off in silence but the farther she drove, the madder she got. Finally as they neared the ranch road she burst out, "I was never more humiliated in my life! Trying to start a fight. Honestly! It would probably have turned into a street brawl. Men have no sense."

Dev let the cool air blow into his face from his open window. The chill wind helped clear the fuzzy mist from his mind. How many beers had he drunk tonight? More than he should have. His stomach roiled and his head ached. However, he knew it was fury rather than alcohol that muddied his thinking.

"You're right about that," he said, his earlier anger now directed at himself.

"Well," she said, momentarily at a loss for words. "I'm glad you realize it. What brought on that ridiculous display?"

"Nothing," he muttered. He wanted to ask her to shut up—his head was nearing the exploding point—but knew that wouldn't be politic in her present mood. She was mad as hell at him.

She swung the station wagon into the final turn. Dev groaned and held his stomach quiet with an effort. The sound of the tires over the bridge roared through his brain with the fury of a freight train at top speed.

When she stopped by the garage he got out and opened the door for her, glad to be back on land. Her angry driving had made the car feel as if it were a ship at sea. He followed her into the house. Now if he could just get to bed without further trouble....

"What gave you the right to take a swing at Anthony?" she demanded after they were in the house. She flipped on the hall light, which hurt his eyes.

"Lainie, could we discuss this in the morning?" he requested.

"No, we could not."

"All right," he muttered through clenched teeth. "He was kissing you. I thought you didn't want him to, so I stepped in and stopped it. Wasn't that what you wanted?" His eyes narrowed as his temper rose again. "Or did you just want to make a fool out of me?"

She propped her hands on her hips. "Oh, I think you did that quite well without any help from anyone else."

"Oh, is that so?" He took a step toward her. The scent of her perfume wafted under his nose as she stood her ground. He felt dizzy with longing. All night he had watched her with other men. All night the demons of envy had eaten at him. Yet he had refused to succumb to the temptation of holding her. A damned martyr, that's what he was, and her flirting with every man in sight!

"Yes," she began. "If you could have seen how you looked—"

He had had enough. To shut her up, he did the only thing a gentleman could. He kissed her.

It started out innocently enough but changed after the first second of contact. He could never touch her without wanting more. He wanted all the sweet taste of her, all the passion he knew she possessed. He gathered her closer until there were no spaces.

He felt her stiffen for a moment, then her arms went around his shoulders and she went up on her toes the way a woman knows how and fitted her body to his.

He was lost to her touch and the sensation of her in his arms. The night, the dance, the jealous fury of a moment ago, disappeared under the onslaught of emotion that gripped him now.

"Lainie," he murmured against her lips. "Lainie…"

He sounded like a man who was drowning and enjoying every minute of it. He sounded like his father. Charles had said Debra's name just like that one time after a quarrel. In his mind he associated it with weakness. A woman could use a man's love against him and bring him to his knees.

Dev pulled his mouth from Lainie's. She stared up at him, her eyes dazed with passion. He could take her, and she wouldn't utter a word, but then what? What would the future hold? He'd be like his father, always yearning for the woman who'd left him.

"Dev," she whispered.

It nearly defeated him to hear her say his name in

a voice husky with desire he had aroused. The awareness had always been there between them—kept
carefully hidden, but there.

He removed her arms from around him. His glance
was one of remorse. Lainie saw that he regretted the
kiss they had shared. He was turning away from her.

''I won't be a slave to any woman, Lainie,'' he
said hoarsely, his face going hard with anger again.
Then, he turned and left.

A few minutes later she heard the thud of hooves
on the hard-packed ground near the stable, and he
was gone, riding up the trail to the ridge.

Chapter Eight

Lainie sneezed four times, then continued dusting the tiny glass animals and replacing them on their glass shelf. Feeling another sneeze coming on, she grabbed for the tissue in her pocket and dislodged one of the brackets supporting the shelf. Fortunately, she caught the shelf before it fell and sent the menagerie crashing to the floor.

She frowned in irritation as she realized that she couldn't hold the shelf in one hand and pick up the bracket with the other. Now what?

The bell tinkled over the front door as someone came in. "Help," she called. "I've gotten into a mess."

Footsteps pounded across the pine planking. Dev rounded a highboy and took in the situation. "Here, let me take that."

"Get the bracket—it's down on the floor some-where—and put it back. Then I can set the blasted shelf on it."

He found the support and replaced it in its metal guide. Lainie eased the shelf onto it.

"Thanks, you were a lifesaver. I thought I'd have to stand here until Tess came back from lunch." Her smile was remote, polite. She had retreated to a friendly distance with Dev.

They had hardly spoken since the night of the dance almost three weeks ago. In fact, she had rarely seen him. He was out of the house before first light and often didn't reappear until after she had gone to bed. Once, when he had returned in the truck around midnight, she had watched him park by the barn and stand looking at the night scene.

He had been dressed in slacks with a white shirt and sport jacket. Agnes had said he had gone to the monthly stockmen's meeting. She remembered how vulnerable he had seemed, standing there alone in the moonlight. Dev, vulnerable? That was fantasy on her part.

"What brings you to town?" she asked.

He looked freshly shaved and showered. His West-ern-style shirt was open at the throat, revealing a patch of thick brown hair that was only slightly darker than the hair on his head. The jeans he wore were old ones, their color faded to pale blue. They clung to his thighs as he bent to check the fit of the bracket.

"That looks okay," he said, straightening. He swung back to her. "I had some banking to do. I thought I'd stop by and see if you needed a hand with anything."

"Everything's fine...now," she added at his slight grin.

"Have you had lunch?"

"Tess is going to bring me a sandwich." He frowned, but before he could say anything she led the way to the front window display. "How do you like the scene? Tess did it. She has an eye for color and design."

A tea table was set in the bay window. It held a lovely pair of cream-colored linens and a china tea service. A pair of gloves lay in a chair. A purse dangled from the arm of another. It was as if the occupants had momentarily stepped into the garden to admire the roses. A screen, inlaid with ivory, formed the backdrop for the grouping.

"Nice," Dev commented, peering over her shoulder.

Lainie repositioned the screen and turned to him. She realized they were very close. He didn't move back to give her room to step around him. She looked up at him, aware of the warmth of him in the confined space.

His face was closed, giving away no thought as he stared down at her, a faint frown etched across his forehead.

"What is it?" She wasn't sure she could stay this close and not collapse into his arms.

"I forgot to tell you that I bought the building, not just the shop. Here's a key to the upstairs part. Dora said there was access from the inside as well as the outside."

Lainie took the key. "There's a door I thought led to a storage room. I was going to call a locksmith to open it. Let's try the key."

They went to the back of the store. She fitted the key into the lock. It turned with a faint *click*. Feeling like the heroine in a murder mystery, she led the way upstairs.

"An apartment," she exclaimed a few minutes later. "I wonder why it hasn't been used."

The place consisted of a large living room that looked out onto a covered porch and a view of the hills behind the shop. A roomy kitchen plus two bedrooms and a bath completed the dwelling.

"I think her son lived here before he married and moved away. You could rent it out—"

"No," she broke in. An idea occurred to her. Why not use it herself? It was certainly handy to her work. And it would get her out of Dev's way at the ranch. "I may decide to furnish it and move in. Look at the view from the living room."

Dev followed her to the windows that lined the back wall. "Live here?" he repeated slowly. "Why?"

She lifted an edge of a heavy drapery. "These

would have to go. I don't want anything blocking the view.'' She glanced over her shoulder at him. ''It would save that long drive every day if I stayed here.'' She would have privacy, she thought. She wouldn't have to guard her emotions the way she did at the ranch.

''What about Tess?'' he asked.

''She could stay here, too, if she wished. Maybe that would be for the best…'' She trailed off, unable to read his thoughts. ''Well, we can discuss it later. I have a thousand things to do this morning. I think I'll decline lunch.'' She smiled brightly and led the way back downstairs.

There she found she had a customer who bought one of the shepherdesses. Only three of the original dozen were left. The woman asked for it to be gift wrapped. Dev tipped his hat to both of them and left.

Lainie answered her client's stream of chatter absently while she affixed a yellow bow to the package and handed it over. The woman left, and Lainie went back to her dusting and arranging, her thoughts on Dev and his unexpected appearance.

Later, while trying to move a narrow hutch, she decided he was probably thrilled with the thought of her moving out. One less female in his hair. The hutch suddenly moved.

''Where do you want it?'' Dev asked.

''There.'' She pointed. ''When did you come in?''

''While you were daydreaming. Here.''

He thrust a bag into her hands. It was from a local

diner and inside were sandwiches and cartons of slaw and potato salad that emitted delicious odors when she opened the bag.

"Lunch," he said. With a grunt he heaved the heavy oak hutch into the space she had indicated. "Anything else?"

"Well," she said, "since you're here and you volunteered…"

A grin tugged the corners of his mouth upward. "I should have my head examined, but tell me what needs to be done."

For thirty minutes she directed him in shifting the larger pieces of furniture so she could form little scenes with them. He followed orders without comment.

When they sat down at one of the tables to eat, she praised him for his patience and ability to take directions. "I thought men who were used to being in charge wouldn't listen to someone else."

Dev laughed ruefully. "With my father, one had to learn to do both…or else."

Lainie felt her compassion stir. "It wasn't easy, wasn't it?" she said in a gentle tone.

He didn't close her out or pretend not to understand. "No," he said. "It wasn't easy, but neither was it impossible."

Lainie bit into her corned beef sandwich while she mulled over his statement. He seemed to be telling her something.

"My father would have eventually accepted you, if you had stayed around."

She looked at Dev, confused by the gentleness in his tone and the hardness in his eyes.

"In fact, he would have loved you."

"Never," she whispered. She swallowed painfully.

"Yes. You just couldn't see it."

The jingle of the bell halted the strained conversation. Tess came in. "Did you tell her?" she asked, looking at Dev.

"Not yet. We got sidetracked." He smiled at Tess, an honest-to-goodness smile, not a sardonic twist of the lips, before looking at Lainie. "Marilynn and some neighbors are going camping up in the national forest next weekend. I told Tess she could go."

"Will you be okay here?" Tess asked anxiously.

"Yes. It's about time you had a weekend off, so go and enjoy." Lainie smiled at her sister, then at Dev, pleased that he trusted the teenager enough to let her go.

Lainie forced her eyes from Dev and fought the hunger that flared that had nothing to do with the food she'd consumed. She glanced up to find Tess' eyes narrowed on her, speculation in them.

"How will you go on this camping trip?" she quickly asked. "Do you take horses, hike or go by car?"

"Marilynn's going to take a truck. Robbie's folks have a Jeep. Hilary and I will go with them."

"Well, it sounds pleasant. I'm sure you'll have fun."

Dev broke in. "We can drive up Saturday night and join them for a camp fire supper. If I know Marilynn, it'll be great."

"No, I think I'll probably work late," she declined.

He shrugged. "Suit yourself."

When he left to go to the ranch and Tess took over dusting and arranging the odds and ends in attractive displays, Lainie went into the office. Instead of going over the books and setting up the accounts the way she liked them, she dwelt on the conversation with Dev. Did he think she had been recalcitrant and unforgiving for not coming back to the ranch?

She recounted her reasons for staying away—to prevent quarrels between Charles and her mother, to keep Dev from being sent away by his father, to…to hold her own emotions in check, she admitted honestly.

Would Charles have accepted her as Debra's daughter and learned to love her? More to the point, would he have accepted her as Dev's wife? Her hand shook as she reached for the coffee cup.

The entrance of several customers ended the tormenting line of thought. She went to help Tess wait on them.

"Hello," one of the women said. "Did you hear about your neighbor?"

"What neighbor?" Tess asked.

"Carson McCumber. I just saw Ethel Asher. She said she saw Carson coming out of the doctor's office with his arm in a sling and a brace on his wrist. Seems he got banged up trying to capture a wild horse over in Sycamore Canyon."

"The Appaloosa," Lainie murmured. "Did he get the horse?"

"I don't know. She didn't say." The woman glanced around. "Say, do you have any more of those Bo Peep porcelain figures? My niece has a birthday coming up. I saw one over at Maud Smith's house…"

"They're over here," Tess said.

Lainie watched her sister. She could see the worry in Tess' golden brown eyes, but the girl was composed as she helped their customers choose gifts for various occasions. Tess was holding her own. Lainie was proud of her.

August was tearing by at the speed of light, Lainie thought on Friday. Tess was off on the camping trip and she found her own activities expanding as she became involved in the Chamber of Commerce meetings. People who had been vague memories from her previous visits became more than faces.

Customers, admiring the way she had done the store, dropped by to chat and ask her advice on decorating. They often invited her to have lunch at their homes and look at a particular problem for them. She found she liked being needed and looked upon as a valued friend.

She glanced out the front window before closing the store. The wind was kicking up, and a storm was building over the ridge of mountain. A colossal storm, she amended, if the size of the thunderheads was any indication. She decided not to linger.

After putting the Closed sign on the door clip, she turned out the lights, locked up and left. Out on the winding canyon road, she gripped the steering wheel as the wind buffeted the station wagon from side to side.

The house was silent when she arrived. Agnes had left supper in the oven. Dev was nowhere around.

Lainie changed to jeans and a long-sleeved knit top. The air was definitely getting cooler as the storm grew. After eating she decided to check the stables and barns. Perhaps Dev needed help.

The stallion was in the paddock. He whickered hopefully when she appeared at the rail fence, then ran toward the stable door.

"What's wrong?" she crooned to him when she led him to his stall. "No one been around to feed you your oats tonight?"

She scooped feed from the bin for both the stallion and the mare Dev had bought from Marilynn. Giving the mare a pat on the neck, Lainie drifted outside. Farther down the creek she could see several head of cattle grazing. In the field beyond the paddocks, the spare horses were gathered near the lean-to, ready to take shelter when the rain hit.

Where was Dev?

The worry she'd been putting off swept over her in a trembling wave. Had he been hurt? Was he lying in a field exposed to the elements? Probably not.

She knew Zed was delivering supplies to the cowboys who were riding herd and checking fences. Had Dev gone out to help him?

The pickup truck had been in the garage when she arrived. Would he have taken one of the remuda horses? Wait! The plane!

She ran around the house until she could see the airstrip along the creek. The plane was gone. He must have flown into Phoenix. He'd probably spend the night due to the weather. She'd be at the house alone.

The wind kicked up a dust cloud around her feet. She retreated to the front porch. The cattle were moving away from the creek. Even from this distance she could tell they were spooked. The hair on her neck rose as a chill ran down her spine.

The drone of an airplane engine halted her just as she decided to go into the house. Her eyes anxiously swept the sky over the ridge, then she spotted it. In a few minutes, Dev set the single engine Piper on the hardpan and taxied to a stop. She ran out to help him tie it down.

When they finished they headed for the house, Dev holding her arm as if he thought she might blow away. When he closed the door behind them, she turned and smiled up at him. "Looks like we're in for quite a blow."

"Tess didn't go on the camping trip," he said. His face looked more dangerous than the storm clouds.

"How do you know?"

"Halfway over the mountain, one of the kids got sick. They thought it was appendicitis and brought him here so I could fly him to the hospital. Marilynn said Tess called and said she couldn't make it because she had to work at the store." He plucked the pickup keys off their hook. "I'll see you later. We might not get back tonight."

"Where are you going?"

Dev paused at the door. "To the McCumber place." He jerked his sheepkskin jacket off its hanger and headed out.

Lainie grabbed a coat from the hall closet and ran for the garage. She climbed in the passenger side of the truck just as Dev started the engine.

"What the hell do you think you're doing?" he demanded. His voice was colder than a winter wind.

"I'm going with you."

He pulled out of the garage with a squeal of tires and tore down the road. Instead of taking the blacktop, he turned onto the gravel road that wound up through the ranch canyon.

"Don't interfere," he told her. "We tried it your way; now we'll try it mine."

She laid a hand on his arm. "It's because she was

worried about him. He'd been hurt trying to catch the wild stallion. I should have realized she would want to see Carson.''

''This will be the last time she does,'' Dev said.

Lainie didn't say anything. Let his temper cool some, she thought. She realized that was what she had always done—backed off and waited for a quieter moment. Cool, calm Lainie, the peacekeeper. What had it ever gotten her?

''I won't let you humiliate her.'' She spoke without emotion, thus making her statement all the more determined.

He flicked her a glance that should have wounded. She gazed back at him, her mouth as set as his.

''Stay out of it, Lainie.''

She shook her head. ''No. I won't let you hurt her.''

The road became rougher, and without four-wheel drive in the pickup, it would have been impassable. They bounced and skidded across chug holes and around narrow curves as they wound their way over one ridge, then another. Night had settled in a light-ning-riddled pall over the land before they spied the lights of a ranch house.

The red Mustang was in the driveway. The wild mustang pawed at the ground in a lean-to. Lainie saw it in a streak of lightning just as the heavens opened up and poured rain upon them.

''Come on,'' Dev said. He had parked behind Tess' car. He flung open his door and waited for her before making the run for the house. The door opened just as they thudded to a stop on the sagging porch.

"Come in," Carson invited. "I've been expecting you." He closed the door against the wind and rain once they were inside. "Hope you brought pajamas. I don't have any."

"We'll go back by the main road," Dev said.

Carson shook his head. "Sorry, but the bridge is out. I haven't had the time, or money, to fix it." He smiled, a sardonic twist of the mouth. "By the time you reach the creek, the water will be up and the ford impassable."

Lainie looked out the window at the slashing rain. He was right. They'd have to spend the night. There was no way they could get back over the ridge road. It would be as slick as grease by now, and with the bridge crossing to the main road out...

"Where's Tess?" Dev demanded.

Carson jerked his head toward the living room. Lainie went first, her heart already aching for her younger sister.

A fire burned in the grate. A bucket caught raindrops that fell from a crack in the ceiling. Tess huddled in a worn chair close to the hearth. She was the picture of dejection as she stared into the flames.

"Are you all right?" Dev asked. His voice was gentler than Lainie had expected.

Carson answered. "Nothing happened."

The two men faced each other, their bodies tense.

"Nothing was going to happen. I would have sent her home in the morning."

"In the morning?" Dev inquired with cynical overtones.

The younger man gestured toward the window. "I just came in a few minutes ago. I didn't know she was in the place until then. I couldn't send her away with the storm brewing."

Tess glanced up at his harsh tone. It was clear that he wanted nothing to do with her. She looked back at the fire, shutting herself off from them. Lainie felt Tess' pain as if it were her own. She took the chair next to Tess' and gently touched her on the arm, then left her alone.

"If you'll excuse me," Carson said. "I'll finish supper."

There was total silence in the room after he left. Dev cursed under his breath. "Why?" he asked.

Tess clenched her fingers together. "I heard he was hurt. I just wanted…to see if he was all right." She flung her head up. "I intended to join the camping trip tomorrow."

"If you expect me to believe—"

Lainie stopped him with a glance. Dev blinked at the fury in the gaze she turned on him. Lainie had never looked at him like that. Until recently. He had rarely been able to read her emotions during her brief visits to the ranch, but now she was quick to reveal her anger when she thought he was wrong. It gave him clues to the depths contained in her.

Watching her cast a sympathetic glance at Tess, he realized how deeply compassionate she was. She was caring, and she was passionate. What else lay hidden behind the quiet facade she exposed to the world?

He studied Tess. No flicker of emotion betrayed her thoughts, either. What was he to do about her? He ran a hand over his face. God, but he was tired. He wished he could go to bed. With Lainie, he thought. He'd like to wake up with her beside him....

And then what? His tired mind taunted the restless desire that strummed through him like current in a high tension wire. Would sleeping with Lainie one time erase a lifetime of wanting her?

He looked at Tess. Was that the way she felt about Carson? He smiled grimly and shrugged out of his coat. Throwing it on the floor out of the way, he crossed the room to the sofa and sat down. It was going to be a long night.

Lainie went to the kitchen after a searching glance at Tess, then at Dev. Carson was spooning soup into thick crockery bowls with his left hand. He cursed as he slopped some on the counter.

"Here, let me help." She eyed the brace around his wrist. "Aren't you supposed to have that arm in a sling?"

He shrugged. "I don't have time to coddle the damned thing. As you might have noticed, there's a lot of work to be done around here."

"Yes. I met one of your hired hands, Anthony Archer, at the street dance."

Carson grinned slightly, and Lainie could see why Tess had fallen for him. His dark eyes and hair, the deep tan, gave him an exotic air like a pirate or bandit. She could picture him as a highwayman with a black handkerchief covering his lower face.

But his eyes were old, she thought. He had had to grow up too soon, too fast. There was bullish determination in his jaw and a dream in his heart. If anyone could make this rundown place a success, he could.

"Tony's my only hired hand. In fact, he hired himself. He's taking his pay mostly in experience. He's going to write a paper on ranch management for his senior project. That was my subject when I was at the university, too."

She was surprised that he had gone to college.

"I had a scholarship," he said, guessing her thoughts.

"Very good," she said sincerely. The more she learned about this young man, the more she liked him. "How old are you?"

"Twenty-four. You thinking of adopting me?" His humor was reminiscent of Dev's, sort of funny, more than a little cynical and somehow sad. He expected nothing from life that he didn't wrest out of it by sheer guts and hard work.

"Umm," she replied. She did have an inkling of an idea. Dev would most likely kill her when he found out. But it could wait. At the moment, Tess was uppermost in her mind. "Tess loves you. Don't hurt her."

The tension escalated from one to ten on the Richter scale. Carson clenched his fists and pressed them against the edge of the counter. "How can I help it? What have I got to offer her—a house the wind blows through, a roof that leaks and a few scrawny cattle no self-respecting coyote would eat? How long would her love last if she had to live here?"

"You and Dev don't give her enough credit for knowing her own mind." Lainie smiled up at him. "She's merely young, not half-witted. Time will take care of that."

He snorted. "It'll take care of a lot of things. She'll meet some dude in college and marry him."

Lainie didn't argue. From the living room she heard the deep rumble of Dev's voice, then Tess' answering monosyllable. She carried the bowls to the table while Carson found a box of crackers and glasses for milk. A pot of coffee brewed on a back burner. He was efficient in the kitchen. He'd had to learn early to take care of himself.

Lainie shook her head at the wave of compassion she felt. Every homeless waif, every broken heart, called forth an answer inside her. She should learn to be tougher.

"Supper," she called when the table was set.

Carson left and returned with his arm in the sling. Dev came in. "Tess isn't hungry," he said.

"I think I'll take a tray in front of the fire," Lainie decided. She loaded an old Coca-Cola tray that Carson gave her with two bowls of soup and a glass of milk and went into the living room. "Join me," she invited, sitting beside Tess once more. "Don't let them see you defeated."

The sternness of her tone penetrated the fog surrounding Tess. The girl took the bowl and ate, her eyes on the fire in bleak despair. When Lainie handed her the milk she drank it down without protest. Lainie knew that at the moment, filled with misery, Tess didn't care about anything, but in a few days, given Tess' natural buoyancy, the girl would spring back.

"Come on, let's see if we can find a bed."

Carson was one step ahead of her. He already had the master bedroom prepared for them. "You'll have to share," he said. He looked at Dev. "You can have that room."

"Where will you sleep?" Lainie asked.

"I usually bunk down in the office." He nodded toward a closed door off the living room.

Lainie insisted on washing the dishes. To her surprise, Tess dried them and put them up before retiring to the bedroom. Carson excused himself and disappeared into the room he called his office. Lainie poured two cups of coffee, handed one to Dev and carried the other into the living room. She sank into the chair with a sigh.

Dev took the one Tess had vacated. "God, what

a day,'' he muttered. He moved his neck in a circle to loosen the tension.

"Here, let me rub your shoulders,'' she said. It wasn't until she stood behind him, her fingers massaging the tense muscles of his neck and back that she realized what she was doing, but she didn't stop.

"Ah, Lainie,'' he said in a husky growl, "you have magic hands.''

When her fingers grew tired of pressing and kneading, she simply stroked them over him. At last he put his hands over hers, stilling her movements. With an easy tug, he pulled her in front of him.

His eyes blazed golden in the firelight. She realized that there was no other light in the room. Outside, the storm raged as if driven by a thousand demons. Wind whipped around the eaves of the house making eerie moans. The rain dripped steadily into the pan on the floor…*plop…plop…plop…*

"Lainie,'' he said. Just her name, nothing more.

She could feel the awareness spinning between them like magic threads, binding them closer and closer. The pain of wanting him caused an ache deep inside her. Just once, she thought, just once. Not tonight, of course, but sometime. If he would only give her a sign of his true feelings.

But it wasn't to be. Even as she hesitated she saw the hardness return to his eyes.

"You'd better go on to bed,'' he said, letting go of her hands. "I think Tess has learned a lesson. She won't come here again.''

"No," she agreed sadly. "She won't trespass where she's not wanted." Neither would she. Dev obviously didn't want her in his life. She would move to town.

Chapter Nine

Lainie stood in the middle of the living room and pivoted in a slow circle, surveying the room. The slate-blue sofa picked up a color in the wallpaper on one wall and echoed the varying shades of blue in the oval braided rug that covered most of the floor. Splashes of coral in the accessories added warmth.

A lounger and two casual chairs completed the grouping. She had arranged the furniture to take advantage of the view from the window. In the winter she would turn the setting ninety degrees to face the fireplace in the end wall.

The rest of the apartment was ready, too. Tess' bedroom was done in yellow and coral, Lainie's in coral and white, the bathroom and kitchen refurbished in blue, again with touches of coral. The place was bright and clean and ready to be lived in. She planned on doing so before the end of the month, which was only a few days away. Tess would also live there during the school year.

My, how time flies and all that, she thought with sardonic humor. August was almost gone. She had gotten totally caught up in the challenge of improving the store. Her efforts were paying off. Business was increasing at a satisfying rate. In fact, she had had to hire a woman to help her out until Tess could come by after school and take over.

Now for the next project. Dev would skin her alive if he found out what she intended to do, but that thought made no dint in her determination. If she could help Tess find happiness, she intended to do it. Carson needed capital to get his ranch on its feet. She intended to supply it.

"Ready to move?" she asked Tess the next day when the teenager showed up for work.

"Yes. Are you?" Tess laid her school books on the desk where she did her homework between customers and other chores. During the past weeks, she had settled down and demonstrated a maturity that made her seem older than seventeen and more than a high school senior.

She was a good hand around the shop. Her ideas on marketing were sound, and she possessed the knack of knowing what their customers would like. Lainie depended on the younger woman's advice for buying merchandise.

"Yes. I thought I would pack tonight and bring

my stuff in with me tomorrow morning. As soon as I finish one more task here, I'm going back to Virginia Beach for a few days.''

''Are you going to sell your house and store?''

Lainie shook her head. She didn't know if she would stay in Arizona for more than the year it would take to get Tess through school and off to college. ''I'm going to lease the town house. The manager at the store is interested in buying in. I think that would be a good move. Maybe I'll buy another shop farther down the coast. There's this place I've had an eye on…''

Tess started laughing. ''You just can't stand it when anything isn't run right. You have to take over and straighten it out.''

Lainie was startled by this insight into her personality. That aspect hadn't occurred to her. Did she try to direct life the way she thought it should go? She had certainly taken over Tess' young life and was about to stick her nose into Carson's life, as well. Lainie, the interloper.

''Can you take over for the afternoon?'' she asked. ''I have some running around to do.''

''Sure. Take all the time you need. I can stay late. In fact, I could spend the night. Hilary would loan me some clothes to wear to school tomorrow.''

''I don't plan to take all night,'' Lainie said dryly. ''That new shipment of stationery is in. You can put it on the rolltop desk if you have time. Don't bother if you have a lot of homework. I'll see you around suppertime. Oh, I'll need your car.''

The two of them rode into town together each morning. "Be my guest," Tess offered graciously, handing over the keys.

Lainie's thoughts reverted to her earlier musing as she drove the red Mustang along the paved road toward the ranch. Dev had said Charles would have loved and accepted her if she had stayed around. Would he? Perhaps she hadn't given him a chance to get to know her personally. Dev had been right. *She* had decided she had to leave the ranch in order for the others to be happy.

Agnes had suggested it was time she took some happiness for herself. How? Could she force Dev to make love to her when he always retreated before things got out of hand between them? Could she force him to love her as she loved him? She shook her head sadly and turned onto another paved road just before the Sycamore Canyon junction.

It was thirty miles farther to Carson's home place. Massive stone pillars, ten feet high, supported a wrought iron sign with the "McCumber" name written in looping script at the entrance. It had recently been repainted.

The ranch had once been prosperous. It would be again if Carson had his way. She intended to boost things along. Tess would be out of college in five years. The ranch had to be ready by then. After that…fate would decide.

When Lainie pulled to a stop in front of the house, a dog ran out to greet her, barking loud enough to wake the dead.

"Shh, quiet, boy. Where's Carson?" she asked, patting it on the head while it looked at her with melting brown eyes. Dogs were so loving and loyal. Maybe she and Tess needed a pet rather than a man. Life would be simpler.

She was still kneeling beside the car and smiling at this idea when a furious male voice demanded, "What the hell do you want? I told you to stay away. Dammit, I have enough problems—"

He stopped with comical abruptness when he rounded the Mustang and saw Lainie petting the dog.

"I thought…I'm sorry…it was the car…" He glanced at the bright red auto, then at Lainie. A dull flush deepened the tan on his ears and neck.

Lainie rose and tilted her head to one side as she gazed up at the tall, thin young man. "That should teach you not to jump to conclusions," she said coolly, but with a smile. She held out her hand. "Hi, I'm Lainie Alder. I don't think we were properly introduced the last time we met."

He stared at her, suspicion in every line of his tense frame. Finally, he shook her hand after he determined that no one else was lurking in or behind the Mustang.

"Tess is minding the store," Lainie said. "She's quite good at it. I think she has a head for business. Do you have any iced tea? It's hot."

"I think there's some in the house. Come on in," he invited, recovering from his surprise at her presence.

Like Dev he watched her without giving any portion of his own thoughts away. Lord save us from inscrutable men, she silently offered as she fell into step beside him.

He opened the screen door and escorted her to the kitchen. She took a seat at the table while he found clean glasses—a real task since most of the dishes were stacked in the sink—and poured them each a glass of murky-looking tea. He peered at the glasses as if uncertain of the quality of the contents.

"I made it last night," he began.

"Tea turns cloudy when it's refrigerated," she told him. "It doesn't change the flavor. You can add a little boiling water to clarify it again if you wish, but I'd just as soon drink it now."

He brought the glasses over, handed her one and took a long drink of his. When he put it down it was almost empty. He wiped the moisture off his top lip with an impatient gesture.

"What do you want?" he asked bluntly.

A younger version of Dev. She blinked back a sudden rush of tears. "I have a business proposition for you." She gave him a cool glance. "Perhaps you'd better be seated."

He took her advice and pulled out the chair opposite her. He turned it around and straddled it. He folded his arms over the top rung and looked at her steadily, waiting for her to begin.

"I'd like to buy a share of your ranch," she said.

Her calm statement hit him like a splash of cold water in the face. "What?"

"I've made some inquiries. You have several thousand acres of good grazing land here and not much else. I think between us we can make it into a going concern once more." She paused for effect. "Like it once was in your grandfather's time."

Carson flung himself from the chair and paced to the back door. He stared out at the rolling land for a minute before turning on her, his hands balled into fists. "Who the hell do you think you are and how did you come up with a stupid idea like that?" His eyes narrowed. "Did Garrick send you over?"

"Hardly," she said.

"Is this his first move in buying me out and getting me out of the country? You can tell him I'm not having anything to do with him or his sister. You can tell him—"

"Will you shut up and listen?" she demanded, breaking into his tirade. Her harsh voice always surprised people. She had learned to use it to her advantage. "Sit." She nodded toward the vacated chair.

"Well?" he snarled when he straddled the chair once more.

"You're broke. I have money. You're a good

rancher. I'm a good businesswoman. I've been studying the market for the past month—''

He snorted at this.

''Pork is taking over a large share of the beef market. You know why?'' She didn't wait for an answer.
''Because it's leaner. People are so fat conscious
these days, they're selecting food largely on that basis. Come up with leaner beef that's also tender and
you've hit a niche in the market.''

''That's been tried—''

''Tender lean, that's what we'll call our beeves,''
she continued as if he hadn't spoken. ''We'll sell
directly to first-class restaurants, aim for the aging
yuppie families with their concern about fitness and
the quality of life. I'll be your marketing manager.''
She stopped and looked at him with brows slightly
raised.

''You're nuts,'' he said.

''A very astute assessment.'' Her eyes narrowed.
''I'm disappointed in you. I thought you wanted to
make this place a success…like the Garrick ranch.''
A hit below the belt, but all was fair in love's on-
going war.

The muscles in his forearms stood out as he
clutched the chair in a death grip. ''I do.''

She had touched an emotional core, she saw. His
voice had been raspy with suppressed feelings. ''So
let me help—''

''Dammit, that's *my* dream you're talking about!''

he glared at her, the urge to smash things evident on his face.

"So let me buy into it," she requested softly.

They stared at each other across the scarred oak table.

"Why?" he finally asked, his voice low and dark.

She ached for him, sensing his pain. This one's for Tess, she silently soothed her own conscience. "Because when the time comes, I want you to be ready for Tess."

His fist came down on the table. "She's nothing to me. She has no place in my life or plans."

"Not now, but later, when she's through with her schooling and learning about the world, she'll want to come home...to you," she added, flinching at her own cruelty as a line of anguish formed around his lips.

He drew a deep breath, let it out slowly. "There's nothing here for her. Tell her that." He stood. "Sorry you wasted your time driving out. There's nothing here for you, either."

Lainie leaned her head back so she could look him in the eye. "There's a matter of a loan that's coming due. You gonna have the money to pay it?"

He was startled, then angry. His face closed, shutting out all expression. "You have been checking around, haven't you?"

"Yes. Your creditor wants his money. I've decided to buy the note. If you won't take me as a partner, you'll have me as your personal loan shark."

She stood and hooked her purse over her shoulder. Stay cool, stay businesslike, she cautioned. Don't show pity. That was the only way to win him over. She understood men and their damnable pride.

Carson stuck his thumbs in his belt and rolled back on his heels. "You want another glass of tea?"

She studied him, wary of his changing mood. "Yes." She sat back down.

He poured them each another glass and took his seat. "Well," he drawled, "how much do you want to come in for, pardner?"

She glanced at him sympathetically. How could she put a price on a dream? "A quarter of a million sound about right?"

"Heard the latest?" Agnes asked, plunking down a breakfast of waffles and sausage in front of Dev. She placed a pitcher of warm syrup within easy reach, then went to pour coffee and milk for him.

Dev finished off a glass of orange juice before he answered. He was hungry and already tired. He'd been out treating a bunch of sick calves before six o'clock that morning. It was now ten and he'd just gotten time for a meal.

He rubbed a hand over his jaw. He needed to shower and shave, then he had business in town. "You need groceries or anything?"

"You going to try eating on a regular basis?" Agnes asked in her barbed manner, faking an interested air.

He scowled at her. "If you hadn't been here since Day One," he threatened halfheartedly, "I'd fire you for being the smart mouth that you are."

She chortled under her breath, her moving shoulders the only outward sign. "You lose much more weight and you'll have to wear suspenders to hold your pants up," she advised.

"Humph," he snorted, pouring syrup over the waffles and taking a big bite. "What was the latest you were so eager to mention?"

"You're probably not interested."

"Agnes."

She laughed again, then gave him the news she'd heard at the bridge club yesterday. "Looks like Lainie plans on staying a while. She bought an interest in the McCumber place. She and Carson signed the papers two days ago."

The bite of waffle Dev was swallowing seemed to enlarge and stick in his throat. He gulped half a glass of milk to get it down. "I'll beat her within an inch of her life," he muttered, his lips thinning against his teeth. "She'll lose everything she owns."

"Finish your breakfast," Agnes admonished. "You'll need the energy if you're planning on starting a fight with Lainie. She's pretty stubborn."

Dev took a bite and chewed furiously. In three minutes flat he was finished and heading up the stairs to the shower. Fifteen minutes later he was on the road. Agnes watched him tear across the bridge with a loud rumble of tires on the metal grid surface, a smile on her face.

Why? he asked himself for the twenty-ninth time as he rounded the curve and turned onto the paved road into town. Why would Lainie do such a damn fool thing? Women! Swear to God, they were the most unpredictable critters ever created.

He gripped the steering wheel of the truck with such force that his fingers were stiff by the time he reached town. He braked and turned into a parking slot down the street from the shop, slammed out of the truck and stomped up the sidewalk. The bell jangled when he threw open the door to Lainie's shop and closed it behind him.

Lainie was seated at an old-fashioned lady's writing desk, balancing her checkbook. She wore a white, high-necked blouse with a cameo brooch at the collar. Her skirt was a soft print of blue flowers on a white background with a flounce of lace showing at the hem. Her hair was up on top of her head in curls. Tendrils hung about her face.

She reached up and absently pushed one behind her ear. As long as Dev had known her, that one strand at her temple had drifted over her face as if determined to be noticed.

He realized she was concentrating so single-mindedly on her task that she hadn't even heard him come in. He crossed the polished planking with a cat's tread and stood behind her to peer over her shoulder.

"Got any money left?" he asked. He heard the sarcastic drawl and saw her back stiffen as she turned to face him, but it was too late to modify his tone.

"Plenty," she said. "You need a loan?"

She looked so cool, so distant—the way she had usually appeared whenever she had visited the ranch—that he wanted to shake her. Or take the pins out of her hair and remove her prim clothing and stroke her until she looked the same as she had the night in the stable.

He realized that their second night in the stable had replaced the first in his memory. There had been more to it, an actual kiss, and later he had kissed her in his bedroom, there on the bed with her hair spread over the sheets, black silk against white cotton.

A stab of longing jolted through him, hot and demanding.

Forget those memories, he warned. He was here on business. Lainie was behaving foolishly, and he was going to put a stop to it. "What possessed you to loan money to McCumber?" he demanded.

She stood, gathered her checks and ledger, and walked away from him, leaving him standing behind her chair like a gauche cowboy with his hat in his hands. He muttered an imprecation and followed her.

"Milly?" she called toward the back. "Would you take over for a few minutes? Dev and I will be upstairs."

Again he was forced to tag along after her. She guided him into the living room and waved toward an easy chair. "Have a seat. I'll make a fresh pot of coffee."

Reining in his temper he took the comfortable chair and, with his long legs stretched out in front of him, surveyed the room. It was the first time he'd been here since the furniture was installed. The room reminded him of the changes Debra had made at the ranch, brightening and warming the rooms with color and light.

"This looks…nice," he said, vowing to start over and talk to her rationally.

"Thanks." She placed a tray on the oak coffee table. Steaming cups of coffee and a plate of apple fritters tempted his appetite. "You look like you could use some nourishment."

He forced a smile. "You and Agnes seem to be trying to fatten me up. I feel like a lamb before Easter."

She took one of the matching chairs opposite him. He noticed that her shoes were the same blue as the flowers in her skirt. A strap was fastened around her ankle, calling attention to its slenderness. He wanted to touch her.

"I saw her in town yesterday. She said you were working too hard. I agree. You seem to be losing weight."

"You've lost some, too."

She handed him a cup of coffee and a napkin. "Then we can both indulge our sweet tooth. Have a fritter. Milly made them this morning and brought them in.''

The conversation was insane. He hadn't come to discuss their weight, but suddenly he didn't want to talk money or business or have a fight with Lainie. He wanted to pull her into his lap, her and her ridiculous old-fashioned get-up, and muss her up. Damn, he shouldn't have come here until he was calmer.

He ate a fritter, then another. It wasn't until she poured them fresh cups of coffee that he broached the subject he had come here to tackle. ''Agnes tells me you've bought into the McCumber ranch.'' His glance asked that she tell him it was a lie.

She nodded.

When she didn't elaborate he felt his fuse shortening. She knew he wanted information and reasons. ''Do you mind telling me why?''

Her lashes rose in the most provocative manner when she looked up at him. ''Yes, I do mind.''

''Dammit, Lainie,'' he roared, losing his temper completely.

''It's none of your business, Dev. You aren't my financial adviser or my keeper. I can handle my own investments.''

He set the thin china cup none too gently on the table and paced to the windows and back. ''You call putting your life savings in a run-down ranch a sound investment? That's bull and you know it.''

She placed her cup on the table with great precision, which made him want to snatch it out of her hands and throw it across the room. He ached with the need for action. He wanted to shake her—no, he'd never touch Lainie in any way that would hurt her, he realized. He wanted to hold her, to keep her safe from all harm, to make her *his*.

She stood and faced him, every inch of her five-foot-six-inch frame stiff with resolve. "I will do what I want with my money. That was not my life savings. I have a million dollars in stocks and bonds. I own half a shopping center on beachfront property in Virginia. I have several units of vacation rental property. Thanks to you, I now own two stores. I have a quarter interest in a ranch which, in five years, will be one of the best in the state of Arizona. Here's my bank balance in my personal account."

She walked to the table where she had deposited the ledger and flipped it open for his inspection. He saw that she did indeed have a very healthy amount in her checking account. More than he had in his, in fact.

"I never realized you were that wealthy," he muttered. "I was worried...I thought..." He stopped, feeling like the fool he was.

"I am a very good businesswoman, Dev. So was my mother. So Tess is going to be. I don't know if it's inherited or what. Maybe Mother and I learned how to handle money because we had to. We were poor after the divorce. She earned a degree and started a career on her own. We learned to invest in the stockmarket together. My mother wasn't broke when she and Charles married. The marriage wasn't the big coup for her that people around here supposed it was.''

Dev realized he had always assumed that Debra had been grateful not to have to work. He'd never thought of her in terms of having a career, but she had been a successful marketing executive. Lainie was right. Her mother had been very good with money. After she'd taken over the books and managed their accounts, the ranch's financial situation had improved. He'd been too young to know why.

He took a deep breath, then smiled. The anger left her eyes, and she looked wary of him. He didn't blame her. He knew when to eat crow. ''I'm sorry,'' he said. ''You're right. It was none of my business. I'll mosey on back to the ranch where this country boy belongs.''

He gave her a wry glance and saw that she didn't look amused. Twin spots of color still blazed in her cheeks; otherwise, her face was impassive. Only the slight trembling of her hands betrayed agitation as she smoothed her skirt. He'd have to eat some more.

''Look, I know I tend to be…overprotective. Wasn't that the term you used?'' When she didn't say anything, he tried again. ''I just didn't want you to get hurt.''

She nodded without speaking.

He couldn't take it. Unable to stop himself he clasped her arms and pulled her closer, forcing her to look at him. ''Talk to me, scream at me, hit me, but for God's sake, do something,'' he demanded between clenched jaws.

"Let me go, Dev,'' she said quietly.

He had to comply. He'd never hold her against her will.

She pressed her hands together. "You've accused me of using your father; my mother, of marrying him for money. You think I hate the ranch. Why did you call and order me out here? It seems your life would be simpler if you ignored me.''

He ran a hand through his hair, fighting the desire to take her into his arms. He felt defeated. "I never thought those things except when I was angry at you, or jealous and wanting to hurt you. I never meant to imply anything about money, except that I was afraid you'd lose all you had. I never thought Debra married my father for anything except love…the greatest, most enduring love I've ever witnessed between two people.''

Tears sprang to her eyes, making them into shimmering blue pools. She covered her face. "Yes,'' she whispered through her fingers.

Dev touched a strand of her hair. He gently brushed it back from her temple. Several truths had dawned on him in the last few minutes. "I never realized what Debra gave up to be the kind of wife my father needed. It just never occurred to me. Until now. I remember her boss at the wedding. He told my father that if he didn't treat her right, she would always have a job waiting at his company. She was the best marketing analyst he'd ever known.''

Lainie lifted her head. ''She understood people and money. That's why she was so good. So does Tess.''

''Yes,'' he agreed. ''A minute ago, when you reminded me of Debra's business degree and investments, I realized several things. She must have put her money into the ranch. Immediately after the marriage, things got easier around here, money-wise. We suddenly had the means to expand and to drill for oil. The cash flow problems disappeared when she took over the books.''

''Mom had invested in the oil venture shortly before the marriage. I think Charles thought it a poor investment.''

Just the way he regarded Lainie's investment in Carson's run-down ranch, Dev thought, his mind still reeling from the new insights. He realized another fact. ''The money from the oil operations should be yours, not just a third of it, all of it.''

She shrugged. ''By the same token, the money from the ranch should be yours and Tess'.''

''No, I think Debra invested in it, too. Damn, this is complicated. I think you should be earning more—''

''It doesn't matter,'' Lainie said, clearly out of patience with the discussion of finances. Like her mother Lainie was smart, but she wasn't interested in money for the sake of being rich. Lainie cared only for the people involved…like Carson and Tess. Dev felt a great tenderness toward her.

He let his fingers glide along the smooth skin of her cheek and under her chin. She was like warm silk to the touch. Heat shattered into burning fragments inside him. "So much caring," he murmured. He heard the huskiness in his voice as his body thickened with desire. "Lainie."

The intimate atmosphere of her apartment was too much for his self-control. He slipped his hands around her waist and eased her against him. She put up no resistance. With one hand behind her waist and the other stroking her face, he held her for a long moment, looking into her eyes. "Why didn't you ever stay?" he asked hoarsely.

"I couldn't. It hurt too much."

"What hurt? My father's jealousy? The love he and Debra shared? What, Lainie?" He needed to know, totally understand why she left them all the time. It was something that had always hurt him, he thought with sudden insight into himself. If Lainie had felt as strongly about him as he felt about her, could she have maintained the distance between them?

"Everything," she moaned, pressing her face against his shirt front. "Oh, Dev, everything hurt then. It does now."

"Why?"

"I wasn't really part of the family," she said. "Your father, you were wrong about that. He would never have accepted me or...or adopted me. I was never one of you, a Garrick.''

''Is that what you wanted to be?''

''Yes. No. I don't know. I needed a family, a place of my own, someone to care for, who cared about me.''

He listened carefully as she tried to explain her needs. He wanted to offer himself, his life to her. He closed his eyes and rested his cheek on her hair. He had learned a lot in the last few minutes. His father had loved Debra, not with the obsessive, sacrificing love he had thought, but with a deep, sensitive need to make her happy. In spite of his feelings, Charles had been as good as he knew how to be to the daughter Debra had had by another man. He had provided Lainie with an education, and he had protected her from his own son's desperate passion for her, even to the point of threatening to send Dev away.

Debra had given up parts of her life for Charles, too. A good marriage meant compromise and changes for both partners. Lainie had probably had that with her husband. He had never found it with anyone.

Lainie had wanted him—still wanted him—but she hadn't cared enough to overcome her fear of his father. No woman had ever given up anything for him.

Gently, he put her away from him. The temptation of her in his arms was too great. He rubbed a hand over his face, pressing away the burning sensation in his eyes. She looked at him with a question in hers.

He touched her forehead, her nose, her chin with the back of one finger. "I've wanted you with a wild passion for years and years, but it's not to be. It takes more than desire to make a life, doesn't it?"

She nodded, the little strands of hair bobbing around her face almost wrecking his good intentions of leaving her alone. She needed to find a future with some man she could love as much as he loved her.

He was proud of himself. He walked away without taking what her eyes were offering. Inside, he felt sadness strike his soul. It was as if a part of him had died. It had. The part of him that held back, that had been afraid to love as his father had loved—totally and without restraint—knew that he had lost his chance with Lainie long ago. It wasn't only that she had left; he had never encouraged her to stay. He had been afraid of loving like that.

Driving back to the ranch he realized that he *could* have had it all. When they had been young together and falling in love, he could have claimed her. Then he would have had more than memories to sustain him for all the years since that time. And for all the years to come, he realized.

He'd never marry. Not now. He'd not put the sadness of unfulfilled love that he'd seen in his mother's eyes into another woman's. And he'd never love another the way he loved Lainie.

Chapter Ten

Lainie signed the lease agreement for the Virginia town house, stuffed it in an envelope and sealed it. It seemed she had signed a lot of legal documents that summer—the lease, the partnership papers on the beachfront store, the loan arrangement with Carson and the title to this building that housed her shop and apartment.

Her glance strayed to the calendar. It was almost fall. September was fast fading into a memory. To-night she had promised Tess that she would go to a fund-raising dance sponsored by her class at school. She felt too old and weary to take part.

Since that strange encounter with Dev almost a month ago, she had rarely seen him. When she had he had acted friendly but remote, reminding her of how she had always behaved around him. But she had been trying to hide her love for him and to protect her mother from suspecting that she was unhappy at the ranch. What was Dev's problem?

A year, she thought, then she would leave and start a new life somewhere else. Maybe Florida. Or California. There was a whole wide world out there. Happiness did not reside in one small corner of Arizona.

The air was chilly. She thought of building a fire. No, she would be leaving for the dance in another two hours. She left the desk and ambled over to the windows. Rain was falling. The line of hills had disappeared in the mist. The entire week since she had gotten back from her business trip to Virginia had been dismal.

The tears fall in my heart like the rain falls on the village. Some poet had written that. French, she thought. She could remember translating it from that language in college. A thousand years ago. A whimsical smile touched her mouth.

She lifted her hand and felt it on her lips. In the glass she could see her reflection, a dim ghostly figure on the pane. Sometimes she felt that way, too. So thin and insubstantial as to be almost transparent. Lainie, the ghost.

She was feeling sorry for herself. Who wouldn't on such a sorry day? She gave a mock glare at the weather. Straighten up, she mentally ordered. The kids need a good turnout for their dance tonight.

The sound of footsteps running up the stairs signaled the entrance of Tess into the apartment. She came in with a rush of cold air and a spray of raindrops as she stopped in the tiled foyer area to brush the moisture from her hair and remove her damp overcoat. "It's cold and getting colder," she announced. "We might have snow before morning."

"That won't be good for the dance, will it?" Lainie inquired, commiserating on the loss of revenue.

"Cowboys'll turn out for a dance through a blizzard," Tess confidently predicted. "Have you taken your bath yet? We need to leave early to help put the food out. Do you mind?"

"Not at all. I was just thinking of heading for the shower when you arrived. I'll get with it."

"You were staring out the window," Tess corrected and smiled her new, grown-up smile that broke Lainie's heart.

The tears fall in Tess' heart, too, Lainie thought. "Only for a minute. I was checking the weather, hoping the rain would stop."

"I'll use the shower after you," Tess volunteered. "I'm going to do my nails now." She disappeared into her room.

Lainie hurried into the bathroom. An hour and a half later they were both ready. Tess wore a short evening dress of sunny yellow with a lace overlay embroidered with flowers. Lainie had chosen a mauve silk dress with stand-up petals over her breasts and a deep blue satin insert in the plunging

V of the neck. Because of the rain she decided on leather pumps rather than the matching satin shoes, but she changed to the blue satin purse. A blue bow was clipped into her ebony hair.

"Your hair looks nice since you've had it trimmed. I like the way it just touches your shoulders," Tess complimented, picking up her purse and extracting the keys to the Mustang.

"Thank you. I arranged for my car to be shipped out. It should be here next week. Then I won't have to borrow yours all the time," Lainie said, putting her raincoat on.

It took only fifteen minutes from the time they left the apartment until they entered the large gym where the dance was being held. A group of senior class musicians was supplying the music, and a tuneful discord filled the air as they tested the tone of their instruments. Lainie helped set out platters of food prepared in the home economics department that day.

"This looks delicious," she murmured, eyeing a tasty dish of tiny seafood quiches.

"Have some," Tess invited. "We didn't eat any dinner."

"I know. I forgot about it."

"Me, too," Tess said.

Their eyes met with understanding. They had grown closer, becoming comfortable living in the same house and sharing problems of school and work. Tess had matured rapidly that summer. Lainie had learned to open herself more to her younger sister, and they had discussed love in all its miseries and glories. Sometimes Lainie suspected that Tess knew who her first love had been, but she was tactful enough not to ask.

People began to arrive for the evening's festivities. The mayor and his wife came in. Anthony ambled in soon after. He was alone. He spotted Tess and Lainie and wandered over.

"Need any help?"

"No, we're finished," Tess told him.

"You two look gorgeous."

"Thanks," both women said in unison.

"Save me the first dance," he told Lainie. "I'll do you second," he promised Tess.

"Okay." She glanced from Lainie to Anthony, then grinned. "If you're sure you can fit me in."

Anthony flipped her on the nose like a playful older brother. At that moment the principal welcomed them to the Annual Senior Autumn Ball. The music started, and Anthony led Lainie onto the floor, almost beating his father, who, as mayor, traditionally stepped out first with the homecoming queen.

An hour went by. Lainie danced with Anthony, his father and several others she had met. Tom, the cowboy she'd met at the Frontier Days dance, twirled her around the floor every time he got a chance. She realized that he had a crush on her. Her smile was unconsciously sweet when their last dance ended. She excused herself and went to the refreshment table. Dev was there.

"Well, hello. I didn't know you were coming. Did Agnes come in, too? I haven't seen her in ages." Lainie realized that she was disconcerted at seeing Dev. For some reason she had assumed he wasn't attending.

"Tess made me buy a ticket," he said. His eyes wandered over her, from the bow in her hair to the shoes on her feet. "No, Agnes didn't feel like coming out in the rain. Said her arthritis was acting up. She was going to sit before the fire."

"Oh." She absently loaded a small plate with goodies.

"Here's a table," Dev said. He led her to one along the wall. They ate in silence. She waited for him to ask her to dance. When he didn't she watched the others on the floor.

"There's Marilynn," she mentioned. The divorcée was dancing with Anthony. Anthony saw her looking at them and winked. When the music ended, he escorted his partner to the table.

"Hey, Dev," Anthony said in greeting. "Let's change partners. Marilynn wants to ask you about some horse."

He whisked Lainie onto the floor just as the band struck up a tango. They performed the dramatic dance with fervor. Lainie knew she was putting on an act because of Dev. An hour later, although he had danced with Marilynn, the mayor's wife and several others, he still had not asked her. At midnight she saw him standing beside Marilynn, his head cocked to one side as if he were listening intently. Suddenly, while she was in the middle of a sentence, he excused himself and walked off. Marilynn was left standing with a chagrined look on her face.

It occurred to Lainie that Dev didn't seem to pay much attention to any women. There was that lovely divorcée, obviously trying to capture his interest and he walked off as though she had been a stranger he had just met. Why?

Putting down the punch cup Tom had brought her, she turned to him. "I need to talk to someone. Excuse me."

She went after Dev and intercepted him before he could take a glass of punch from the girl who was serving. "Come on. You haven't danced with me yet."

With a slight frown he followed her out to the dance floor and took her in his arms.

"Are you enjoying yourself?" she asked, putting on a bright smile. Did his eyes look haunted, or was that her imagination?

"Yes." He glanced at her, then away.

"Why haven't you ever married, Dev?"

It was unfair to hit a man with a question like that in a public place, but she suddenly had to know. He was a handsome, virile man. She knew he was passionate. But he had never been linked with any one woman, although she knew he had dated occasionally. At one time she suspected that a certain widow had been his mistress, but he was discreet and, of course, had never confided in her. She was filled with curiosity. Her nerves hummed with energy that had deserted her of late.

His hands tightened on hers, then relaxed. He smiled with a rakish twist to his lips. "Never found a woman who'd have me."

She knew that was a lie. Marilynn was evidence of that. Lainie also knew there was no use questioning him. He wasn't going to confess the secrets of his heart there on the dance floor.

After the dance he escorted her to a table where Anthony beckoned. The young man swept her into his arms, and they danced to the melody of a Strauss waltz. From the corner of her eye she saw Dev watch them for a minute, then he went to the cloakroom, retrieved his coat and left the dance.

Emptiness descended on her like a hailstorm, leaving little pieces of her shattered. Without the tension and excitement of his presence, she felt half alive. Without him, she was less than complete. Dear God, why was love so difficult?

A vision of his face as he had stood watching her and Anthony dance rose to haunt her. There had been longing in his eyes. From inside her, like a dam bursting, other perceptions flooded her mind, drowning out logic and leaving only gut feeling to guide her.

Dev had always wanted her, but he had always held back. Why? If all he felt was desire, why did he withdraw at the last minute? It certainly wasn't because his father would send him away now. Why not take what they both wanted and be done with it?

Why?

The question burned and prodded. She looked at Marilynn and thought of Dev's lack of interest in the woman. It was as though, for him, she didn't exist, not as a potential lover or wife.

Why?

Or if he weren't interested in Marilynn, there were other women who would have loved a chance to be part of his life. Lainie knew he was family oriented. He was not a promiscuous person, yet he had established no long-lasting relationships.

Why?

She battled the driving impulse that urged her to leave the dance and confront him. She sensed the minutes passing by and felt that each one was a precious moment lost for all time. *'Bout time you took some happiness for yourself,* Agnes had said. She went to find Tess. "May I borrow your car?"

A flicker of distress passed over Tess' face before she answered. Lainie turned to see the cause. Carson had just come in. He paid for a ticket, although the dance was less than two hours from being over, then stood by the back wall and glanced around. His eyes stopped when they rested on Tess.

"Yes," Tess said, a curtain coming down over her face. She nodded at Carson, then looked away.

"Can you get to the apartment if I don't return to the dance?"

"Where are you going?" Tess asked, puzzled by Lainie's urgency.

"After Dev. I think it's time we had a talk."

"Lainie?" Tess questioned, realizing something of import was about to happen.

Lainie smiled grimly. "You've guessed, I think. I love him. Tonight I mean to find out how he feels."

Tess handed her the keys. "Go for it," she said. Her smile was tremulous. "I thought there was something between you two. Don't let him say no." She glanced at Carson, then away. "Be happy," she whispered.

"Thanks, love." Lainie hurried across the room, forgetting her raincoat.

Carson stepped forward. "Good evening, pardner," he said with his devil-may-care grin on his face.

"Can you see Tess home if I don't get back before the dance ends?" she asked, hardly pausing. She must hurry.

The grin disappeared. He glanced across the room at Tess, who was dancing with Anthony just then.

"Oh, come on. I don't have time to explain," Lainie snapped. "Will you or not?"

"All right. If it's important—"

"It's my whole life," she said and sailed past him.

The drive out to the ranch was endless. The rain beat against the windshield, blocking out the road more than a few feet in front of the car. When she turned onto the ranch road, she gasped as a flying figure dashed in front of her.

The wild stallion raced toward the canyon beyond the ranch. He had gotten free. She wondered if Carson knew. She heard him trumpet, not in challenge but as if questioning. An answer came, but not from Dev's show stallion. It was the mare destined to establish the dynasty. She followed the wild horse up the trail and they both disappeared from sight.

An omen, Lainie thought and didn't laugh at her superstition. Her hands visibly shook when she stopped in front of the ranch house and removed the keys from the ignition. She dropped them in her purse, opened the door and raced through the rain for the house. *'Bout time you took some happiness for yourself.* The words drummed in her head like the drops of rain on the ground.

She stopped inside the hall and brushed the water from her face and hair. There didn't seem to be a light on anywhere, only a faint glow from the den. She laid her purse on the parson's bench beside the door, for the first time realizing that she'd left her coat at the dance. On trembling legs she walked silently down the hall.

Like a thief she crept silently to the open door and peered inside. Dev was there, sitting in front of a flickering fire, his elbows resting on his thighs, his hands hanging idle between his knees. He looked so handsome, so masculine...and so alone.

The firelight gilded his profile and emphasized the broad sweep of his shoulders. Such dependable shoulders. Such a trustworthy man.

Dev, her first love and her last.

Chills rushed up and down her spine, collided in the middle and scattered to all parts of her body. She felt hot and cold by turns as she walked silently into the room and stood near the sofa. Would he never notice her? And what should she say when he did? She had no words planned.

He checked the time on the clock on the mantel, sighed, then stood, full of restless energy. Shock registered on his face when he saw her watching him in the gloom.

"What the hell?" he said.

Not exactly the most welcoming words, but about what she'd expected. She smiled. The smile trembled a bit upon her lips. She licked them and hoped the action was provocative. She'd never tried to seduce a man before.

"Hello, Dev," she said, making her voice soft and enticing. She was probably making a total fool out of herself.

His face became as impassive as those at Mt. Rushmore. Only the hard throbbing of a pulse at the base of his neck gave her encouragement. She moved closer to him and let her breast brush his arm, just a tiny bit, once, then twice and yet a third time. It was a blatant invitation. She didn't want her intentions to be misinterpreted.

He looked somewhat stunned. A sardonic smile touched his lips while he shook his head. "I must be dreaming."

"Let me share the dream," she pleaded softly. She sat on the sofa and patted the cushion beside her. "Let me stay with you tonight."

"Why?" The word was a hoarse croak.

"Because it's something I think we deserve. We've always…wondered how it would be. I want to find out. I want *you*."

The evidence of his arousal was not easily hidden even by his slacks. He didn't try. "Lainie, we can't." He closed his eyes against the invitation in hers.

"Why not? We're adults, Dev. We know what life is about—"

"Dammit, you don't know at all," he ground out.

"So tell me." She gazed at him in challenge.

He sat on the edge of the sofa, at the end away from her. Something in him seemed to crumble and fall, like a barrier giving way. He sighed in defeat. "Because I've dreamed of you so often that way. If that dream becomes reality even once, I'll spend the rest of my life wanting it again."

She reached out a hand and laid it on his arm. The muscles tensed under her fingers. She caressed him, loving the feel of his flesh against hers. "What's wrong with that?"

"What's wrong?" he practically snarled at her. He flung her hand off. "I won't go through life like my father, yearning for some woman who's left me.

When we were younger…maybe I had a chance with you then, but I let it slide by. Now I want everything, Lainie. Not just sex, but…'' He stopped and made a hopeless gesture.

"Love, Dev?" she asked, going breathless with hope. "A life together, a home and family? I see no problem with that."

There, she had all but proposed to him. She waited.

He studied her. A light flared in his eyes as she met his gaze levelly. The hunger rose, and he let her see it. She bit her bottom lip and waited.

"No problem?" he asked.

She shook her head. "It's exactly what I want…with you."

"And you'll stay here and be content, the way Debra was?"

Lainie smiled at him, seeing his doubts, but also seeing more, much, much more. "Yes."

"And never leave?"

"Never."

"You always did before." He leaned slightly toward her. "You hated it here."

"No," she murmured. She lay against the sofa pillows, letting her head loll back so the long, smooth line of her throat was clearly visible. *Hussy.* "I wanted to stay, but so many things seemed to be in the way—my mother's happiness with Charles, his threat to send you away because of me—"

"You knew about that?"

She nodded, her eyes never leaving him. "This was your home. If anyone left, it had to be me."

He came to her then. He gathered her close, and his flesh warmed her clear through like a magic blaze. "I should have known," he muttered. "I should have known. You never kept away because of my father's attitude toward you, or because you hated the ranch. It was other people you were thinking of—my father's happiness, your mother's, mine—never your own. I should have realized." He rocked her gently. "Noble Lainie, always giving."

"Don't make me out to be a heroine. I'm just a woman like any other, Dev." She looked at him with her heart in her eyes. "I've loved you all my life."

"You married someone else."

"I needed someone to love, someone who loved me," she explained. "There had never been anyone for me—"

"I was there," he said in a fierce whisper. He rubbed his face against her hair. "You could have come to me."

She couldn't bear the agony in his voice. With all her might, she hugged him to her. "Not then. But now...tell me you love me. Dev, I need you to love me." A week, even a day ago, she couldn't have opened herself to the kind of hurt his rejection would bring, but now she couldn't stop.

She felt him stiffen in her arms, and her heart sank. Had she asked for too much?

His lips moved against her neck. "I love you more

than life itself,'' he said, the words so low, so harsh, so hard to say. ''I thought you would never be mine.''

''Dev!''

He lifted his head. ''It's true, Lainie. I only realized it recently.'' His smile was a little off center. ''I realized a lot of things recently.''

''About us?''

He moved his hands along her sides. Her pulse beat so loudly in her ears that she could hardly hear his husky voice. ''About life. About loving and what it means. About my father's and your mother's love for each other.'' He looked at her, a desperate need in his eyes. It matched the need in her. ''I still can't believe you're here in my arms. I'm afraid you're going to be snatched away, and I'll be lonely again.''

''I won't leave,'' she assured him.

''I may ask for more than you want to give,'' he warned with fierce possessiveness. ''There are so many things I want for you, from you…all those things you mentioned and more. Mostly, I want *you*, just you, only you, always you.'' He touched her breast and felt for her heartbeat, timing its rapid pace.

''Dev, I can't think when you do that,'' she gasped.

He shifted, then stroked her with only the tips of his fingers touching her, sliding over her thighs, her stomach, back to her breasts. With a fascinated expression he watched what happened to her nipples when he touched them. They rose, visible against the material of her dress and bra.

He grinned at her. "I think we've done enough thinking, Lainie...darling," he added, as if he were trying it on for size. It seemed to fit. "Darling," he repeated. "I've wanted to call you that for a hundred years."

He stood and shucked out of his slacks, his body virile and ready. He looked at her, and his gaze was so hot that she thought she'd go right up in a puff of smoke. He started to unbutton his shirt.

"Dev, Tess is—" she said, remembering the dance and Carson.

He dropped to his knees and gathered her into his arms. "No more talk. We can straighten out all the details tomorrow. Right now..." He nuzzled along her cheek until he found her mouth. His kiss absorbed her words.

It was bliss and ecstasy. It was wildness and turbulence. It was honey and spice. Wild. Sweet. Heaven.

"What were you saying?" he murmured when they came up for air.

"Carson is going to take Tess to the apartment."

"Oh." He kissed her some more. With a gentle nudge of his hand, he opened her legs and pressed his hard body between her thighs. He gazed at her with a tender expression. Sudden realization leaped into his eyes. "To your apartment? Alone?"

She nodded.

"Nothing will happen," he said. "Carson won't let it. He's honorable." He looked at the intimacy of their bodies and groaned. "He's a man."

Lainie smiled.

"Damn."

She laughed and nibbled his ear.

"Tease," he growled. He ground his hips against her, drawing a moan of pleasure from her. "I suppose we'd better head for town. The dance will be over in thirty minutes." He eased himself away from her and pulled on the discarded slacks. "It's just as well. If I make love to you now, I won't let you out of here for a week. We'd better get married first. Tomorrow."

"I'd like a wedding at the church and a reception here, maybe a big barbecue cookout. What do you think?"

"That it'll take days of planning to put something like that on. If you think I'm going to wait..." He looked into her eyes...and melted. "Yeah, if that's what you want."

Lainie rose and put her arms around his neck. "Thank you, my love."

He buried his face against her neck. "Say it again."

She understood. "My love. I love you so," she whispered, fierce and hurting with the force to it.

"That's all I need to know. Let's go to town." He spied her shoes and handed them to her. "One week, not a day longer.'' He looked at her once more, a slow, hungry perusal. ''No more memories after that. We'll have the real thing.''

''For the rest of our lives,'' she promised.

Chapter Eleven

The mare strained one last time. The foal slipped free. Dev cleaned its face and checked that it was breathing. He let the mare sniff and examine it before taking an old towel and rubbing it dry. "A filly," he said.

Lainie started laughing.

"It isn't funny," Dev said in disgruntled tones.

The foal had the unmistakable signature of the Appaloosa on its rump—nicely rounded spots about hand-size. "I get to keep her."

That was the deal. If the mare foaled from the wild stallion, the offspring was hers. If the foal was from the show horse, then Dev trained it for the ring and sold it.

"I hate people who say I-told-you-so," he grumbled.

"The words never left my mouth."

"You were thinking them."

She laughed again and let her breast rub lightly against his shoulder. He finished drying the foal and helped it stand. It dipped its head under its mother and found the teat. Before it could suckle, it lost its balance and tumbled to the straw.

"Hmm, she knows where the good things in life are," Dev remarked. He turned suddenly and Lainie felt her world swirl as he lifted her into his arms. "You've teased me long enough. Now you pay the price, Mrs. Garrick." He strode toward the last stall in the dim stable. It was after midnight.

"Oh, I didn't mean it. What price?" She pressed against his chest and looped her arms around his neck.

"You'll see." He carried her into the stall. Fresh straw was covered by a foam pad, a blanket and a sheet. Two pillows lay at one end.

"Nothing like roughing it," she commented.

He let her slide out of his arms to stand in front of him. With deft fingers he began on the buttons of her shirt. "I don't want to scratch this delectable dish."

In a minute he had her undressed, and in another, he joined her. Sure of his welcome he lay with her, finding the special place that just fitted him. He held his weight on his elbows, careful of crushing her and the child that stirred within her.

Lainie gazed up at her lover, her husband of nine

months, and smiled. He looked content, happier than he had a year ago when she had come back to the ranch at his insistence. The joy of life glowed in his eyes, as well as the flames of desire. The laugh lines were deeper around his eyes.

"My love," she said.

He answered the tenderness in her with an equal measure of his own. "I've wanted to make love to you in here for about seventeen years," he murmured. "I decided I'd better grab my chance before we're inundated with little nosy ones."

He bumped rhythmically against her, filling her with sheer delight. "This was a preplanned seduction. I can tell," she said, trying to sound indignant.

He smiled, then suddenly looked serious. "I'll never forgive my father for driving us apart. All those years lost, Lainie."

She caressed his face, his shoulders. "I think he was afraid that you'd suffer the longing he'd felt for my mother when she was gone. He was trying to protect you." Her memories of Charles were kind. She could never fault him for his love of her mother. It had been too great—like the love she and Dev felt for each other. "We have it all now, my darling."

"Yes. On stormy nights, while we're gathered around the fire with the kids, I'll tell the story of how I schemed all those years to tumble you in the hay."

"You wouldn't," she said, half believing he would.

"No," he agreed, looking happy and carefree and

younger than his years. "This is our memory, yours and mine." He patted her enlarged abdomen. "He'll have to make his own."

Then he kissed her, and they made love while the rain fell on the land and the mare whickered to her newborn.

* * * * *

SPECIAL EDITION™

Emotional, compelling stories that capture the intensity of living, loving and creating a family in today's world.

Modern, passionate reads that are powerful and provocative.

nocturne

Dramatic and sensual tales of paranormal romance.

Romances that are sparked by danger and fueled by passion.

SDIR07

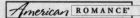

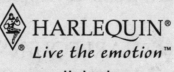

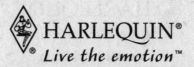

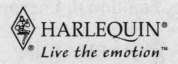

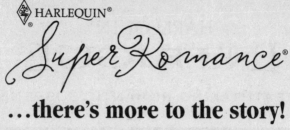

HARLEQUIN®

SuperRomance®

...there's more to the story!

Superromance.
A *big* satisfying read about unforgettable
characters. Each month we offer *six* very different
stories that range from family drama to adventure
and mystery, from highly emotional stories to
romantic comedies—and much more! Stories
about people you'll believe in and care about.
Stories too compelling to put down....

Our authors are among today's *best* romance
writers. You'll find familiar names and talented
newcomers. Many of them are award winners—
and you'll see why!

If you want the biggest and best
in romance fiction, you'll get it
from Superromance!

Exciting, Emotional, Unexpected...

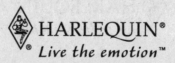

HARLEQUIN®
Live the emotion™